I0609871

# The Atlantis Allegiance

## Book 2

*The Atlantis Saga*

# S.A. Beck

This is a work of fiction. Names, characters, organizations,places, events, and incidents are either products of the author's imagination or are used fictitiously.

ISBN-13: 978-1987859249
ISBN-10: 1987859243

# Contents

# Chapter 1

MAY 27, 2016, SAN FRANCISCO,
CALIFORNIA

11:15 AM

Jaxon Ares Andersen lay curled up on her bed at the Forever Welcome Group Home on the outskirts of San Francisco, knowing her life was over. A group of strange military men was hunting her, and the only other person who knew— her boyfriend, Otto—had been sent off to prison for something he hadn't done.

Now she was alone.

Not that *that* was anything new. She'd always been alone, shuffled from one group home or foster home to another, never settling down, never fitting in, never making friends. Always the odd one out. Always different.

Over the last few weeks, her life had finally been lit by a ray of hope. She'd started coming out of her shell. She'd even gotten a boyfriend.

How pathetic. Her first boyfriend at sixteen. Most girls had them at twelve. She didn't even get to kiss him.

And now that he was in prison for arson, it didn't look as though she'd get the chance.

Jaxon buried her face in her pillow. She had been stupid to think this place would be any different. Every place always ended up being the same. Some looked more promising than others, like the Spencer family that took her in when she was nine. They'd been really friendly, and look how that turned out.

She winced and pushed that memory aside. No point in thinking about that now. Any place that had given her a bit of hope had always disappointed her more than the obviously crappy places.

She had more important things to worry about. Who had those men been? Why were they after her? They had attacked her and Otto in the greenhouse. When she and her boyfriend had fought them off and run away, the strangers burned the greenhouse to hide the evidence. The group home staff assumed Otto had gone back to his pyromania. That was what had gotten him institutionalized in the first place, and lighting another fire counted as breaking his parole.

Those men would come back, Jaxon was sure of it. They must have been after her because of her special powers. Why else would they go after a screwed-up teenager? The real question was—how did they even know about what she could do? No one else, not even her therapist, had any idea.

They'd timed it perfectly too. While there was a security camera in the green-house to make sure no one got up to anything there, no one had been watching it because everyone was gathered on the lawn for visitors' day.

So what should she do? Run away? Where? And do what?

Jaxon sighed. It was hopeless.

A snide voice cut through her thoughts. "Sooooo... how's the love life?"

Lizzie.

Obnoxious, stuck-up, and the dominant girl at the group home. She always had all sorts of little groupies flocking around her. Weak people who wanted to feel big by hanging out with the class bully. From the faint snickering Jax heard, at least two of them were standing in the hall with Lizzie.

"Not so proud now, huh?" Lizzie went on. "Looks like lover boy was a real criminal. Too bad he didn't burn you down with the greenhouse."

"Go away," Jax grumbled. "You're boring me."

"I'm boring? That's a laugh! You're the one with no friends and a boyfriend in lockup. Hope you don't have a little convict baby in nine months."

Jax had a fantasy of leaping off the bed, picking it up, and throwing it at Lizzie. She could do it. That was a big part of the problem—that she was some sort of superhuman freak, like something out of a comic book. Lizzie didn't know about that, of course, or she'd never poke fun at Jaxon. She must sense Jax was different somehow though. People like Lizzie always could.

"What's the matter?" Lizzie continued in a singsong voice. "Not going to the gym anymore? Guess it isn't so much fun when lover boy isn't around to set your heart on fire."

Lizzie laughed at her own joke. Jax, with her face still buried in the pillow, rolled her eyes. Why did stupid people always think they were clever?

"Fine. Just stay in your room. We don't want to see your ugly face anyway."

Lizzie's groupies tittered. Jax heard their footsteps recede down the hallway.

She sighed. If she was going to be lonely all her life, couldn't people at least leave her alone?

A couple of minutes later, there was a soft rapping on her doorframe.

"I said go away," Jax grumbled.

There was a laugh, and Ginger Edwards's voice said, "This is my room too, you know."

"Oh, sorry," Jax said, sitting up and looking at her. "I thought you were someone else."

"I sure hope so," Ginger said with a smile. She walked into the room and sat on the edge of Jax's bed. "How are you feeling?"

"Like pond scum," Jax said, flopping back down.

"That's better than you were feeling a couple of hours ago, and I'm going to make you feel even better. I have good news."

Jax gave her an ironic smile. "You've discovered my birth parents, the judge let Otto go, and Lizzie fell on her face and had to have her jaw wired shut?"

"Um, not quite. I heard from my caseworker, and she says that she's found you a placement in a foster home."

"Already?"

Ginger had told Jax she'd call her caseworker about Jax less than a week ago, just after Otto was taken away for supposedly burning the greenhouse. Jax had been in the system all her life, and it never worked that fast. Ginger's caseworker must have all kinds of connections to be able to work that fast.

"Yup. They're coming tomorrow."

Jax sat up again. "No way!"

"My caseworker says they're really cool. She couldn't tell me much, confidentiality and all that, but she did tell me they're rich."

Jax didn't care about that. This place was no longer safe. She felt a tug of regret to be moving again though. How many times had it been? She'd lost count. The Forever Welcome Group Home had been pretty cool, and she had hoped it would mean something better for her life, but deep down, she had always known it was too good to last.

"Hey, Jax! Don't fall over yourself thanking me!" Ginger laughed.

"Oh, sorry. Thanks. I mean it. Just bummed about having to move again."

Ginger gave her a sympathetic look. "You poor kid."

That made Jaxon giggle. When Ginger called her or the other residents "kids," it always made her sound older, like one of the staff members or Jaxon's therapist, Dr. Hollis.

"Come on," Ginger said, "I'll help you pack so you'll be ready to go when they come."

Jaxon looked from her half of the room, which was neat and tidy, to the disaster area on Ginger's side.

"I think I can handle it." Jaxon said.

She got up and started sorting her things. Packing had become second nature to her, and she didn't need to think about what she was doing. Instead, her mind whirled from the impact of knowing she was getting whisked away, probably never to see Ginger or any of the other kids again.

It was a shame. She had actually begun making friends here, or at least people who would speak to her without laughing at her. She'd miss that.

This place wasn't safe anymore though. She had to get out of there. Yet the question remained—if those guys from the greenhouse could track her here, couldn't they track her to her new foster home?

Would she ever be safe?

# Chapter 2

MAY 27, 2016, SAN FRANCISCO, CALIFORNIA

12:15 PM

Dr. Anthony Hollis couldn't believe his eyes. He'd received an email from the California Child Protective Services informing him that Jaxon Andersen was being reassigned to a foster home.

That didn't make any sense. Jaxon hadn't been at the group home long enough to significantly advance with her therapy. She was just beginning to come out of her shell socially and hadn't progressed at all in her one-on-one sessions with him. He got the feeling she was hiding some secret about herself from him. The girl's intelligence rankings were off the charts, and she had seemed to be engrossed in some strange experiments in the greenhouse, at least until that juvenile delinquent boyfriend of hers burned it down.

Dr. Hollis bit his nail. He could lose his job over that one.

Right now though, he was more interested in what was going on with Jaxon. The teenager's social worker, Helen Jenkins, had moved heaven and earth to get her assigned here, and now she was moving her out.

A new message popped into his inbox. It was from Jenkins. He opened it, and his eyes went wide as he read her lengthy complaint about Jax being reassigned over her head. Jax's new social worker was someone Dr. Hollis had never heard of. Jenkins wanted to know who had spoken with Child Protective Services and whose decision it had been to move Jax into a foster home. She even flatly accused Dr. Hollis of trying to get rid of Jaxon because of the greenhouse incident. Jenkins seemed to think that

Hollis blamed her for not keeping Jaxon in line.

He sat back in his seat, stunned. What was going on?

Dr. Hollis went upstairs to the sleeping quarters. Propriety and state law demanded that he didn't enter the girls' wing, so he asked another girl to go fetch Jaxon.

Jaxon came out after a minute, her face a mask.

"Hi, Jaxon, how are you doing?"

The girl shrugged. "Okay, I guess."

*Communicative as always, I see.* "Let's go for a walk," Dr. Hollis said.

They went downstairs and out into the center's expansive back garden. Not far off lay the blackened remains of the greenhouse. Dr. Hollis studied Jax's face as the ruins came into view. She bit her lip and looked at it with obvious worry.

"I got a strange email from CPS. Apparently you've been reassigned to a foster home."

"I know," she said, nodding.

Dr. Hollis stopped. "You know? But your social worker didn't even know."

"I... called someone at CPS I know and got it squared away."

"Jaxon, this sort of request has to go through Mrs. Jenkins."

Suddenly Jaxon grew angry. "What difference does it make? There's nothing for me here. You sent Otto off to jail!"

"Jaxon—no, don't turn away—you have to understand something about Otto. He's very sick. As you know from group therapy, he's addicted to setting fires. That's what got him assigned here as a condition of his parole. This sort of sickness is a deep-rooted addiction, just as bad as alcoholism or drug abuse. It's a shame he slipped on his therapy and broke his parole. I really thought he was making progress. Unfortunately, it's out of my hands now."

Jaxon stood facing him with a defiant stare, her arms crossed. "He didn't set that fire."

"Jaxon, I know you two were close—"

"We were attacked, I told you!"

Dr. Hollis inclined his head. "Jaxon, you know that there was a video camera in there." He nodded toward the ruins. "We record all our CCTV just in case there's an incident. I looked at the tape, and it stops a couple of minutes before the start of the fire. The fire crew discovered that the cable running to the camera had been cut, and they found a pair of garden shears lying nearby. Otto didn't want to get caught."

Jaxon looked confused. "No, you don't understand. They must have done it so you wouldn't see them!"

Dr. Hollis studied her. She seemed to be in earnest. Did she actually believe what she was saying? She hadn't shown any signs of being delusional, but that could be a difficult pathology to detect if the delusions weren't too outlandish.

"Can I go now? I have some packing to do," Jaxon said, looking sulky.

Dr. Hollis sighed. It appeared this was out of his hands too. He'd have to make inquiries with CPS. He didn't want this sort of thing to happen again. How could he help a young person's mental health if they could disappear at any moment?

The next day, Jaxon's new foster parents showed up, along with Jaxon's new social worker, Olivia Mahone. Dr. Hollis had looked her up and found out she had just moved to California from New Mexico. Jaxon was her first case in the state. Even stranger, the foster parents had never been foster parents before.

As he ushered them into his office, he studied them. Mahone was a mousy, middle-aged woman who seemed to know her business. The foster parents, Stephen and Isadore Grant, were quite a couple. Stephen Grant looked in his mid-fifties, yet fit and handsome with a bearing that spoke of a military background. He had brown hair just beginning to go grey at the temples. Although he dressed casually, the quality of his clothes and the gold Rolex on his wrist spoke of considerable wealth.

Isadore Grant was simply stunning. Perhaps ten years younger than her husband, she looked as if she had been a model in her youth, and perhaps still was. She had Grecian features, crystal blue eyes, and luxuriant brown hair that tumbled over her narrow shoulders. Like her husband, she appeared fit and had a strange seriousness, as if she had been in the military too, although she didn't fit the type. Dr. Hollis flushed as she looked around his cluttered and disorganized office with obvious distaste.

"Please, everyone have a seat," he said, before realizing that all the seats except his own were piled high with books and papers. Flustered, he cleared off three chairs, sending a cascade of papers from one of them. Individual sheets wafted in the breeze coming in through the open window.

Isadore Grant whipped out a hand and snatched one from the air before it flew out the door. The movement was so fast and precise, it reminded Dr. Hollis of a cobra striking.

Once he had cleared the chairs, everyone sat, and he fetched the sections of Jaxon's file the foster parents were allowed to see. That did not include reports of his one-on-one sessions or reports from her earlier therapists. Those were confidential.

"Here you go, Mr. and Mrs. Grant," he said, handing them over.

The couple leaned over the first page of the file with obvious interest.

"Jaxon Ares Andersen. Odd middle name," Dr. Hollis said.

"The ancient Greek god of war," Stephen Grant said.

"Is that what it means? Well, she is a fighter," Dr. Hollis said and chuckled.

Isadore Grant pointed with a slim forefinger and tapped Jaxon's photo with a well-manicured nail painted deep red. "Quite a distinct appearance too. Not a beauty, but certainly someone who stands out of the crowd."

Dr. Hollis looked at the photo. Jaxon had brown skin, yet her features seemed more Caucasian with perhaps a bit of Asian heritage. Her jet-black hair was naturally straight, as far as he knew, and her most distinctive feature was her startlingly blue eyes with a slight Asian epicanthic fold, the irises encircled with a faint brown ring.

"There is no record of her birth parents. She's obviously mixed race though. Is that a problem?" Dr. Hollis asked.

Stephen and Isadore looked shocked at the question.

"Why would it be?" Isadore asked.

"Well, it shouldn't be," Dr. Hollis said. "Unfortunately, it's an issue with some foster parents. Personally, I don't think anyone who has a racial preference is fit to be a foster parent, but the state isn't interested in my opinion."

"A child is a child," Stephen Grant said. "We'd accept her in our home even if she wasn't human."

Dr. Hollis chuckled then stopped as he noticed Isadore give her husband a sharp look.

"Well…" Dr. Hollis coughed. "Once you've read through all this, we'll have some forms to fill out, and then you can meet your new ward."

He studied the paperwork as the Grants filled out each page. He noted that Isadore Grant worked in insurance and Stephen Grant was a leading botanist at UCLA. That was a good fit for Jaxon. She had an obvious talent for growing plants. He couldn't get over that footage of Jaxon touching plants and them growing an inch or more in less than a minute. Dr. Hollis still hadn't figured out how she did that. Perhaps her foster father would have better luck.

"I see you're a botanist," Dr. Hollis said.

"Plant toxicologist, to be exact. I study plant poisons," Stephen said, busy with the paperwork.

Dr. Hollis resisted the urge to frown. Did this guy think he didn't know what "toxicology" meant? "Hmm, yes. Well, Jaxon has quite a talent with plants. She seems to be working on some sort of growth serum, although she never talks about it."

Stephen Grant stopped writing and looked up. "Is that so?"

Dr. Hollis nodded. "I'm hoping that living with a botanist will bring out her natural talents."

Both Grants smiled.

"We'll make sure she reaches her full potential," Stephen Grant said.

Half an hour later, Jaxon stood with her suitcase on the driveway of the Forever Welcome Group Home, looking forlorn and resigned. Dr. Hollis felt sorry for the kid. She had been in this situation far too many times. It was a shame she had to uproot herself once again. At least she was getting a nice place, judging from the airport limo Stephen had called to pick them up.

Stephen and Isadore stood next to her, telling her about the room she'd have in their home in Los Angeles. Jaxon didn't seem to be listening. The social worker stood a little apart.

Frustration and a sense of helplessness rose in Dr. Hollis's chest. This shouldn't be happening. Why had her social worker been replaced? Why this sudden change in Jaxon's placement? Why hadn't he been consulted?

The limo pulled up the driveway. A uniformed driver got out and tipped his hat to them.

As the driver opened the back door, Dr. Hollis turned to Jaxon. "Best of luck, Jaxon. I hope you find some happiness at your new home. If you need anything, you have my number. Feel free to call me anytime."

"Okay," Jaxon said in a tone that told him she wasn't even considering it. The girl was so used to leaving that everyone here was already fading into the past.

Mahone shook hands with everyone, got into her own car, and left. A minute later, the limo pulled out.

As they disappeared around a bend, Dr. Hollis realized that other than signing the appropriate forms, the new social worker had done and said nothing beyond what was absolutely necessary. Usually someone new on a case had a whole string of questions for him. It was only natural.

Dr. Hollis bit his nail. Everything seemed in order. The message from CPS had been clear enough. Something nagged at him though. This didn't add up.

He'd have to do some more research on Olivia Mahone, and more research on Stephen and Isadore Grant.

# Chapter 3

MAY 28, 2016, SAN FRANCISCO, CALIFORNIA

3:30 PM

Jaxon lay back in her first-class seat as their plane took off from San Francisco airport, headed for Los Angeles. She took a deep breath. Another move. Another set of fake parents.

She studied Stephen and Isadore Grant out of the corner of her eye. They seemed okay. A bit cold, but at least they didn't come on with all that false friendliness like some foster parents did on the first day. "Welcome to the family!" "You're our daughter now!" God, how many times had she heard stuff like that? So lame. A bit of coldness made for a nice change, although it did make her wonder. People took on foster kids for two reasons: they needed the money the state gave them or they wanted to feel good about themselves. The Grants obviously didn't need money—who paid for first-class seats for a one-hour flight?—and they didn't seem to get all mushy about having a kid in the home.

So why had they picked her? And why was this done over Ms. Jenkins's head?

Jaxon watched as the ground fell away, buildings and cars becoming like miniature toys. She felt a spike of fear as she wondered if the Grants were like the Spencer family who had taken her in when she was nine.

That had been when a lot of her troubles began.

The Spencers had seemed nice at first. Mrs. Spencer had been friendly and helped Jax with her dyslexia, patiently coaxing her to do her homework as the letters floated in confusing patterns before her eyes. Mr. Spencer had been friendly too, always taking her on long walks in the woods and swimming with her in the pool. If he hugged her and stroked her hair more than the other foster parents had, she didn't think much of it, figuring that was just the way he was.

Then one night she learned the truth.

It was half an hour after bedtime, and she was almost asleep. Mrs. Spencer was out of the house, leaving her alone with Mr. Spencer. A sound in the hallway outside her open bedroom door made her open her eyes.

Mr. Spencer's silhouette took up much of the doorframe, lit by the dim hallway light. Jaxon figured he was just checking on her and closed her eyes again. She didn't hear him walk away.

Just as Jaxon was drifting off to sleep, he entered the room. At first, when he sat at the edge of her bed, she thought he was checking to see if she was asleep. Then he slipped his hands under the covers and tried to pull off her pajamas.

She screamed and slapped his hand away. There was a sharp crack. Mr. Spencer howled, staggering back and holding his wrist.

Her memory was hazy after that. She remembered Mrs. Spencer coming home and Mr. Spencer claiming that Jaxon had tripped him as he was going down the stairs, causing him to break his wrist. The ambulance arrived, then CPS, and she was hustled off to a group home.

That was the first time her unnatural strength had manifested itself. At nine years old, she was too confused and scared to tell anyone what had happened. She didn't even say anything when a caring social worker asked if Mr. Spencer had really fallen down the stairs. Her mind was still trying to register the fact that she had broken a grown man's wrist with a simple slap.

So she got a new label. She already had "learning disabled," "poorly socialized," and "withdrawn."

Now she had "violent."

Nothing like a label to make you second-guess yourself.

Since then, she had been tempted to use her strength so many times. Luckily none were like the incident with Mr. Spencer, but she'd encountered no shortage of bullies, angry foster parents, racist remarks on the street, and cruel pranks against the new kid in class. She could have left a trail of dead people in her wake. She could have killed every one of her tormentors, and there were times when she was seriously tempted.

She wasn't that kind of person though. That's what she kept telling herself. Even if everyone laughed at her for being different, even if she would never fit in, she was never going to be one of the bad ones. She could be something better.

Jaxon realized she was gripping the armrest of her seat. She forced herself to let go and saw the impressions of her fingers pressed into the hard plastic. She quickly covered it up with her arm and looked over at Mr. and Mrs. Grant.

Just in time to see Mrs. Grant looking away.

Had she seen? Jaxon stared out the window at the distant land below. No, she told herself, Mrs. Grant hadn't seen. Jaxon had been hiding in plain sight for so long, she was beginning to believe the whole world was blind. People sensed she was different, but no one could see she was special. Her new foster parents would be no different.

An hour later, they landed in LAX. The Grants ordered another limo to take them home, and they cruised in comfort all the way there.

Jaxon gasped as they pulled up to a beautiful home in a rich area of the city. The house was simply stunning. It was a huge Classical-style mansion with white walls that gleamed in the California sun. As the driver pulled up a broad driveway flanked by spreading oak trees and flowerbeds bursting with color, she saw the wraparound colonnaded porch. A wide green lawn spread luxuriantly on all sides, and the nearest house stood far away. Jaxon estimated they had five or six acres of land. Between that and the house, the property must have cost them a couple of million at least.

"Wow, what do you guys do for a living?"

"Disaster insurance," Isadore Grant said with an enigmatic smile.

"Lot of disasters, I guess, huh?" Jaxon said, shaking her head in wonder.

"More now than ever before," Isadore Grant replied. "Perhaps you'll get into the family business."

Jaxon bit her lip and said nothing. *So you want me to think I'm part of the family already? Right. I've heard that one before. It's not like I'm even going to be here more than a year before the system sends me somewhere else.*

The limo stopped at a walkway leading up to the front door. As they got out, Jaxon saw a large greenhouse in the backyard. Excitement and pain mingled in her. She had loved her time in the greenhouse back at the group home, yet it had been the place of her worst memories too.

*Poor Otto. I wish I could see him again.*

Stephen Grant came up beside her. "I see you like my greenhouse. That's where I do my experiments."

"I thought you were an insurance salesman."

"No, that's Isadore. I'm a botanist, although I guess I'm in disaster insurance too. We have to save the earth from destruction. Maybe you can help. I heard you have quite the green thumb."

Jaxon shrugged. While she cared about the environment as much as anyone else, she just didn't see what she could do about it.

"Come on in," Isadore said, heading up the stairs as the limo pulled away.

Jaxon followed, dragging her suitcase. Stephen came after with the rest of the luggage. Jaxon passed through the front door and gasped. A huge front hall, painted white and decorated with a variety of potted plants, greeted her eyes. A grand curving staircase led upstairs.

"Let me give you a tour," Isadore said. "Steve, will you take the suitcases upstairs?"

Stephen nodded, took Jaxon's suitcase, and headed up the stairs.

Isadore inclined her head. "This way."

They passed into a large living room that had floor-to-ceiling windows over-looking the backyard and greenhouse. The furniture was all of Danish design, with clean, precise lines. A few minimal-ist paintings hung on the walls. Jaxon suppressed a smirk. A couple of years ago, one of her foster families had taken her to a modern art museum, and it had been filled with pointless stuff like this. They were modern stuff made up of single rectangles of one color, or a few lines splashed every which way across a canvas. Most were signed and looked like originals instead of prints. Jaxon wondered how much the Grants had paid for them.

The décor reminded Jaxon of Isadore—high class and impersonal. She suspected that Mrs. Grant had the real money in the family. The only flair in the room was some more potted plants, no doubt a human touch provided by Mr. Grant.

They carried on to a dining room with similar décor and a long, rustic table that looked like an antique. A weird bronze sculpture sat in the center. It was made up of big globes attached by little rods and a couple of spikes sticking out of it. Jaxon saw a title engraved on the base—"Consciousness Rising IV."

Jaxon couldn't keep from giggling. What a dumb name.

Beyond lay the kitchen with marble countertops and clean steel utensils hanging from a rack above them.

"Hungry?" Isadore asked without warmth and apparently without concern.

"I wouldn't mind some fruit juice or something."

"How about a smoothie?"

"Sure!"

Isadore went over to a huge bowl containing every kind of fruit Jaxon knew and a couple she didn't. They looked tropical and rare, probably shipped in special to some high-priced boutique. Isadore grabbed an armful of fruit, peeled them with a few expert cuts from a knife that looked five times bigger and sharper than she needed, and put everything in a blender.

"We live a healthy, natural lifestyle here," Isadore explained as the blender made a loud hum. "Lots of fruit and raw vegetables, and everything is organic. Our meat is all free range."

"Um, okay."

Isadore studied her. "You're probably not used to that sort of diet."

Jaxon laughed. "Institutional food isn't exactly the best, and some of my foster parents weren't all too good in the kitchen."

"I am." Isadore gave Jaxon one of her cold smiles and flicked off the blender. She poured some of the smoothie into a glass and handed it to Jaxon.

Jaxon took a sip. It was delicious.

"Like it?" Isadore asked.

Jaxon got the impression that saying she didn't wouldn't go down well. Luckily she could tell the truth.

"It's great," Jaxon said with a dutiful nod.

"Healthy too. We'll put you on a diet that will get you in prime health."

Jaxon looked down at her body self-consciously. "Am I getting fat?"

Isadore laughed. "No, you're a lovely girl, and from what I've heard, you're quite the athlete. With a carefully monitored diet, we can bring out your true prowess."

Jaxon took another drink of the smoothie to hide her smirk at being called "lovely." She was anything but lovely, as every girl in every school she'd ever been to had made sure she knew. Still, she shouldn't be too hard on Isadore. The woman was just trying to be nice. She was a bit weird, but if she prepared food like this all the time, living here wouldn't be so bad.

"We live as free from modern distractions as possible," Isadore said. "You won't find a TV in this house, and while we can't avoid having computers, we use them as little as possible. Could you put your cell phone on the counter, please?"

Jaxon took out her phone and placed it on the counter, staring at Isadore curiously. Her foster mother picked up Jaxon's phone and put it in her pocket.

"What are you doing?" Jaxon demanded.

"As I said, we avoid the distractions of the modern world. You don't need this."

"But it's mine!"

Isadore fixed her with her cold blue eyes. "If you need to make a phone call, you can ask me for it. Is there anyone you need to call?"

Jaxon flushed. Isadore had a point. Who would she call? Mrs. Jenkins wasn't her social worker anymore, Otto must have had his phone taken from him when he got locked up, and Dr. Hollis wasn't her counselor anymore. Who did she have to call?

She thought back on all the schools and group homes she'd been to, all the roommates and foster brothers and foster sisters, all the study partners. None of them had kept in touch. Jaxon couldn't remember anyone even offering except for Ginger, and Jaxon wasn't about to call a few hours after saying good-bye. That would look totally pathetic. Jaxon looked at the floor.

"Jaxon, is there anyone you want to call?" her foster mother repeated.

"No," Jaxon mumbled.

"That's settled then," Isadore said with a flat smile. "Now let's go upstairs, and I'll show you the rest of the house."

Jaxon followed her, dejected. She knew there would be something wrong with this foster home. There always was.

On the other side of the main hall was a gym. Jaxon felt a tug of nostalgia seeing all the weights and machines. Working out with Otto and his friends had been one of the few good times she had enjoyed in the past year. Now that was all gone.

Isadore indicated all the equipment. "We have a holistic view of education. In addition to enrolling you in a leading school, we'll also work on training your body. Dr. Hollis said you enjoy the gym. We'll get you in tiptop condition."

She led Jaxon to the main hall again. They ascended the broad, curving staircase to the upstairs hallway. Like the rest of the house, it had white walls, a bare wooden floor, and sparse decorations except for a few bits of modern art. Jaxon looked around. The place didn't look very lived in—everything was too clean and orderly. It was like one of those houses in a magazine.

Isadore showed her the bathroom, the upstairs lounge, Stephen's office (off-limits), Isadore's office (off-limits), the Grants' bedroom (off-limits), and finally her new bedroom.

Jaxon wasn't surprised to see that it was large and mostly empty. She had a queen-sized bed, a desk, an ergonomic metal office chair that swung around, a bookshelf filled with all sorts of books, a walk-in closet that was completely bare, and big windows that, when she parted the lacy white curtains, revealed a wonderful view of the backyard and greenhouse. Her battered blue suitcases sat at the edge of her bed. Stephen stood outside the greenhouse door, and when he saw her looking, he gave her a wave and a smile.

Jaxon waved back and forced the edges of her mouth upward.

"I'll let you get settled," Isadore said. "Just let me know if you need anything."

Once she left, Jaxon stuck her tongue out at the empty doorway. *Get settled? Yeah, right.*

She flopped down on the bed, feeling glum. She had slept in homier rooms in institutions than in this mansion. She didn't even have any decorations on the walls. She decided to talk to Stephen and Isadore about that and immediately realized that would be a bad idea. They'd either say no or put up some of that ugly modern art. It was weird that these guys had so much money but couldn't set up a nice house.

At least the bed was comfy. Maybe she should just sleep until she was eighteen.

Isadore's voice called from downstairs. "Jaxon! Once you're finished up there, come on down. We'd like to talk to you about your work schedule."

Jaxon groaned and forced herself to sit up. "Home sweet home." She sighed and started to unpack.

# Chapter 4

MAY 30, 2016, ALBUQUERQUE, NEW MEXICO

1:10 PM

General Hector Meade flipped through the latest Top Secret dossier that had been sent to him from a little-known office at the Pentagon. The public wasn't aware that office existed at all, of course. Even most of his fellow generals only knew of it as an unlikely rumor. The existence of the Extraterrestrial Evidence Bureau was on a strictly need-to-know basis.

General Meade needed to know.

The dossier contained the usual radar tracking data and some long-distance photos taken by powerful terrestrial cameras. They showed what he had seen so many times before—irrefutable evidence that a variety of strange craft had shown up once or twice a week from various points in the solar system to circle the earth for a couple of orbits and occasionally dip down into the stratosphere.

The craft flew faster and farther than anything produced in the United States. There had been talk at the Bureau that the craft might be some super-advanced foreign government or a secretive team of leading scientists, but their spies had found no evidence of either. Those theories didn't make sense anyway. No one on Earth could make a craft that could fly from the dark side of the moon to low Earth orbit in five hours—not the Japanese, not the Russians, no one. Clone an army of Steven Hawkings and they still couldn't do it. It would take decades of research and development.

Centuries, more likely.

So the most plausible explanation was that extraterrestrials existed. Some egghead at the Bureau had suggested the crafts were manufactured by future humans who had mastered time travel and come back to visit their own past, but that was a bit hard to swallow. General Meade had looked at enough intel to know the simplest explanation was usually the correct one.

He'd also seen enough battlefields to know that once your enemy had surprised you, you'd better wrap your head around whatever they'd done and deal with it, or you would get fried. Like that nasty skirmish he'd been in back in 1991, in the frozen sea north of Siberia. A team of Navy Seals, Army Rangers, and Russian Spetsnaz had gone up there to suppress a rebellion by the Russian Mafia, who'd threatened to break their portion of Siberia off from the rest of Russia. They wanted to claim the oil and natural gas in the region, and they had enough Soviet-surplus nukes to do it. The secession would have led to a nuclear civil war in Russia just as Communism was going through its death throes.

The mobsters had drilled holes in the ice, climbed inside, and covered the holes with tarps covered with a thin film of water that quickly froze. When Meade and the others parachuted into what everyone thought was empty terrain, the mobsters broke through. Meade's team had been caught in a withering crossfire,

Americans and friendly Russians dropping all over, until Meade had grabbed a flamethrower and started blasting the craters. The mobsters drowned in the melted ice, which promptly refroze in the -40° temperatures.

For all he knew, they were still up there, entombed in the ice.

That would have made a good story— the last battle of the Cold War saw Russian and American troops fighting side by side to destroy an army of Russian mobsters.

Of course that story never made it into the newspapers of either country.

Neither would this UFO threat. Think of the panic. Think of the religious nutcases. No, the general population could never know they were being spied on by aliens.

Meade had no doubt that was what those beings were doing. As strange as it still seemed to him, he had to accept the fact that Earth was being spied on in preparation for an invasion.

The techniques of military reconnaissance didn't change from culture to culture, and there was no reason to believe they would change from species to species. The flight paths of the UFOs over the past few years supported his theory. The crafts orbited the earth in a regular search pattern in order to cover the entire globe. Whenever the craft came closer, reaching the upper limits of Earth's atmosphere, they invariably did so over sensitive military bases such as missile silos or Air Force testing sites. As far as the Bureau could tell, they did it with all the other highly militarized countries too.

The aliens had even helped them out once. Radar had picked up a silver disk hovering a mile over a secret base in North Korea. The Bureau had already heard rumors that the North Koreans were building a crude atomic bomb, and the aliens' interest led the Bureau to send a tip to the CIA about what the rogue state was up to. They told the CIA spooks the intel had come from a Korean defector. Meade wondered how the CIA's Korea bureau would have reacted if they knew the report had been written in a secret Pentagon office using intelligence based on UFO flight paths.

General Meade shook his head in wonder. He never used to believe in aliens. Back in the eighties, when he was a young and fast-rising officer, he'd been stationed at Holloman Air Force Base near White Sands, New Mexico. It had been one of the test centers for the then-secret Stealth Bomber. The Stealth had caused no end of UFO sightings. It made sense—the plane looked unreal, just a big black triangle. No one had ever seen a plane like it before.

He and his buddies at the base got a big laugh reading the local papers every time some wide-eyed rancher or camper reported seeing an alien ship. The idiots always embellished the tale too. One guy claimed the craft had bloodshot eyes that looked at him; another said it shot out a purple tractor beam that sucked up one of his cows.

Nobody ever said, "I saw a strange airplane. Is the Air Force testing something?"

He supposed that wouldn't make as good of a story. Got to sell papers, after all.

When the Stealth's flight crew came to the base Halloween party dressed as alien Greys, Meade thought it was the funniest thing he had ever seen.

He wasn't laughing now.

There was no way America could fight against such advanced technology, even if the whole world allied with them, which it wouldn't. If the aliens invaded, humans would be crushed like the Conquistadores had crushed the Aztecs and Mayans. Steel swords and muskets against flint spears and stone clubs. Spaceships and God-knows-what weaponry against Stealth Bombers and intercontinental ballistic missiles. The civilian government would probably cut its losses and give up after the first battle.

General Meade wasn't the quitting kind. They had one chance to beat the aliens, and it was almost as unbelievable as the aliens themselves.

The intercom on his desk buzzed.

"What is it, Major Jefferson?" he asked.

"Agent Melody Crown to see you, sir," Jefferson's gruff female voice replied over the intercom.

General Meade nodded. And here was that unbelievable chance, punctual as usual.

"Hold on," he told his assistant.

He closed the dossier and put it in the safe in his office, which he locked. Agent Crown knew a lot of things most people didn't, but she didn't know about the spaceships buzzing overhead. She didn't need to know. The general ground his teeth. Being briefed on so much privileged information used to make him feel special. Now it was giving him an ulcer. Ignorance really was bliss.

Sitting back down at his desk, he jabbed the buzzer. "Let her in."

An automatic lock on his door clicked open. Agent Crown stepped into his office. At only twenty-eight, she was the youngest of his operatives and looked even younger. Her red hair was styled in the latest fashion for high schoolers, and her petite body and youthful features made her look as if she was no more than eighteen.

That could be very handy on some missions.

"Agent Crown, welcome back to the world of adulthood. Please take a seat."

"It's good to be back, sir. Living in that group home with a bunch of juvenile delinquents was beginning to make me feel crazy myself."

"Not the usual sort of assignment for an operative, yet an important one, I assure you. How's the subject?"

"Jaxon Andersen is depressed at how things turned out, and obviously afraid of having to move again. She's resigned to it though. You've read her dossier. This is how her life has always been."

"The Grants will give her stability until she is ready."

"I haven't met those operatives."

"You might have to. Jaxon has bonded with you, and it could be useful to exploit that. The Grants are a husband and wife team and two of my best agents. We're lucky to have them, seeing as they have to play husband and wife for the next couple of years."

Crown nodded. "I can see how that would be useful. So they'll be honing her abilities?"

"Yes. Of course they'll have to pretend not to know about them at first. They're subtle though, good at long-term infiltration. We've used them to wheedle into the confidences of people far more suspicious and dangerous than Jaxon Andersen."

"She's lonely, the poor thing, like all those kids. If the Grants go softly, she'll open up soon enough. As suspicious and jaded as she is, she's dying to bond with someone."

"The husband will be good for that. It's a stroke of luck he's a botanist. They can bond over weeding the garden," General Meade said with a derisive smile. "His wife will have to learn to warm up though. She's one of our best assassins. Raising a surly teenager without snapping her neck will be more of a challenge for Isadore than icing foreign diplomats."

A flicker of concern passed over Agent Crown's features. "They're not going to hurt her, are they?"

General Meade shrugged. "The training will be rough once it starts in earnest. Don't worry though. People with the Atlantis gene are hard to hurt."

Agent Crown shifted in her seat. "If I may ask, sir, is Atlantis just the name for this project or is it... because the subjects are descended from the people of Atlantis?" Crown blushed, turning her freckled face scarlet and making her look even younger. "It's a silly question, I know, but considering what these people can do..." She studied the general, waiting for an answer.

He decided to give her half of one. "I'm not at liberty to say."

Agent Crown sat back in her seat, her jaw slack with wonder. There was a moment's silence as they studied each other.

General Meade decided to break it first. "Did you give the subject your number?"

"Of course. I told her to call me whenever she wants. If she goes silent, I'll text her to say hi. She's a bit shy, so I might have to maintain the contact."

"Good. She's still not on any social media?"

Agent Crown shook her head. "She doesn't have any friends, so being on Facebook or Twitter would only depress her, the poor kid."

"That poor kid is potentially the salvation of this nation, along with the rest of her kind."

"From what?"

"You know better than to ask that."

Agent Crown stiffened. "Yes, sir."

"Keep up the good work, agent. Keep in touch with the subject, and we'll call you when we need you."

"Yes, sir," Agent Crown said as she got up.

She was from the CIA, a civilian agency, so she didn't salute. General Meade sensed she got some satisfaction from that. As she left the room, the general rubbed his jaw and considered the situation. A bit soft, that one. Civilian agents usually were, although the CIA had a few real thugs on the payroll. Meade preferred military agents, ones with training he understood. Finding a soldier who could pass for a teenage girl hadn't been possible though.

The problem was, the civilian agencies had their own agenda. CIA, FBI, Homeland Security, BATF, and a dozen other agencies all vied with one another for funding and didn't want to risk their chance at the limelight by sharing any information. All covert operations would run better if the military maintained sole control. With an alien invasion coming, the military should be running the entire country.

General Meade got up. He had a meeting with some brass at the Pentagon. His superiors wanted to know the results of the Poseidon Project. They were complaining that the project was progressing too slowly and had threatened to pull the plug. Those bean-counting bureaucrats didn't understand that this wasn't like bombing some rogue state. You didn't get results in twenty-four hours. The project would take months, years, to achieve fruition. General Meade wasn't a scientist, but he had worked with enough of them to know they ran at their own pace and you could only hurry them up so much. Sloppy science was no use to anyone.

The general gritted his teeth as he went out the door and locked it. He had to make those idiots at the Pentagon understand. His project was the best hope for this country, and he wasn't about to let anything get in his way.

# Chapter 5

MAY 30, 2016, LOS ANGELES,
CALIFORNIA

10:45 AM

"So, like, what are you anyway?"

The tall blond girl stopped Jaxon in the hallway by stepping right in front of her. Jaxon recognized her type immediately. She was another Lizzie, another Amanda, another Natalie. Wherever Jaxon went, the Queen Bee would sniff her out as different and make sure everyone knew it.

Not that it was hard at this school. Jaxon was the only one without lily-white skin. And that, of course, was what this girl's question was about.

Jaxon sighed. "So what's your name this time?"

The girl screwed up her face. "What kind of spaz question is that? My name's Courtney, everyone knows that."

"I'm new here. I don't know who you are, and I don't care."

Courtney let out a little laugh. "Yeah, but do you know who *you* are? You look like a Chinese and an Indian got squashed together and rolled in the mud!"

A leering crowd had gathered, as usual. Now Courtney would find fault with everything about Jaxon—her different looks, her clothes, being the new kid, and probably a few made-up things too. The crowd would laugh and join in with the popular girl, and Jaxon would have to use every bit of her self-restraint to keep from popping the girl's smug, empty head right off her shoulders.

That was how the first day of school always went down.

In public schools, the race thing never came first. Apparently with rich white kids, it wasn't so taboo. They all looked so respectable, didn't they? The young men and women of Hidden Hills Academy. Clean faces, straight teeth, boys in blazers and ties, girls in green plaid skirts. Little rich brats.

"You didn't answer my question," Courtney taunted. "Where are your parents from, some refugee camp or something?"

Jaxon flushed. She hated questions about her family.

"Her mom's white," one of the other girls said. "I saw her drop her off this morning."

"That's not my mom," Jaxon said. *Oh crap, I can't believe I let that slip.*

Courtney wore a confused expression. Jaxon suspected she got confused often. "So wait, some other woman drives you to school? They don't let your real parents out of the refugee camp?"

"Enough already," Jaxon said, pushing past Courtney.

As her shoulder collided with the little snob's, Jaxon realized she'd put too much force into it. Courtney spun around and fell against the girl next to her.

"Ow! Watch it, mongrel!"

Jaxon hurried through the crowd, which parted to let her past. She went around the corner and to her locker to collect her books for her next class. Great, she'd been at her new school for all of about two hours and had nearly gotten into a fight already.

She still could. Courtney and her crew were tromping down the hallway after her, a crowd of curious kids following in their wake.

Jaxon stared back at her locker, heart pounding. *Don't hit her. You've got to lie low. You found a safe place for the moment. Courtney isn't your real problem—it's those guys who attacked you. They're the real danger.*

*But can't I hit her just once? Why am I always the one who has to show restraint?*

"Hey, you!" Courtney shouted.

Jaxon turned to look at her.

Just then, Courtney's face transformed into a bright, fake smile. "Welcome to our school!"

Jaxon stared at her. "Huh?"

A teacher walked by.

"Oh," Jaxon mumbled.

The bell rang for class. Jaxon grabbed her books and hurried down the hall. As she did, a guy her age fell into step beside her.

"Don't mind Courtney. She's an idiot," he said.

Jaxon glanced at him. Blond. Cute. Rich. Could be Courtney's brother.

"Tell me something I don't know," Jaxon grumbled.

The boy laughed. "My name's Brett."

*Courtney. Brett. Next I'm going to meet Chad and Britney.*

"I'm Jaxon."

"Cool name. Sorry about all that racist crap she said."

"I didn't hear you objecting," Jaxon snapped.

Brett laughed again. "Courtney's totally tweaked out. You can't talk to her about anything. Half the time she doesn't even hear you. Most people can't stand her, but she's popular because she supplies the..." Brett held one nostril shut and made a big sniffing noise with the other.

Jaxon stopped. "She's a coke dealer?"

Brett's eyes widened. "Say it a little louder! I don't think they heard you in the principal's office."

"Don't worry, I'm not a narc. I have enough trouble in my life as it is."

They stopped outside Jaxon's English classroom.

Brett glanced in the room, where all the students were taking their seats, and back at Jaxon. "So... um... do you like golf?"

"Golf?" she asked. What a weird question. If that was supposed to be a pickup line, it was the worst she'd ever heard.

"I'm the captain of the school golf team."

"There's a golf team?"

Brett looked at her as if she was the one who had asked a weird question. "Yeah, wasn't there one at your old school?"

"No, and I don't care, because golf is boring."

Brett looked her up and down and smiled. "You're not boring though. I can tell. It's going to be interesting having you around."

Jaxon glanced into the classroom. Everyone was sitting now, and the teacher was giving her a sharp look and tapping her pen on her desk.

"Got to go," she said, trying to summon a smile.

"See you soon," Brett said.

Jaxon went into the classroom and took a seat. As the teacher droned on, she seethed over the scene in the hallway with Courtney. She hated the first day at a new school. It was always the same—some obnoxious girl would start in on her.

Why was it always like that? In this school she stood out, so it was more understandable, but wherever she went, it was the same. In public schools, the black kids and Asian kids rejected her as much as the white kids. It wasn't just that she was mixed race either, because the mixed-race kids rejected her too.

Race really wasn't what it was about at all. That just happened to be the easiest thing for Courtney to pick on. No, it was something else. Somehow Jaxon broadcast to the world how different she was. It was like she had a big neon sign on her forehead saying MISFIT.

Why? For years, she had tried to fit in and never could. Her words never came out right, or she went about making friends all the wrong way. And then there were times when she was made to stand out, like when kids talked about their parents or grandparents. Even when someone asked something as simple as "Where are you from?" she was set apart.

Jaxon had been a foundling. She didn't have a birth certificate. The courts had decided to designate her "birthday" as the day she had been found at the door of some clinic in San Francisco. Her bassinet had had her name written on it and nothing else. Doctors had estimated her age, and that was what they put on her paperwork. She had a seventeenth birthday coming up, and she knew she wasn't turning seventeen that day. She might be seventeen already, or she might be sixteen like her paperwork said. She might even be fifteen.

How could she fit in when she didn't know anything about herself?

The teacher's voice interrupted her thoughts. "Ms. Andersen, would you mind answering the question?"

Jaxon looked around. The other kids were all staring and snickering.

*Great, the misfit just screwed up again.*

"Um, sorry. Could you repeat the question?"

\*\*\*

At the end of the day, Isadore picked Jaxon up in her Lexus.

"So how was the first day of school?" she asked.

"Great!" Jaxon replied, putting on a smile. "The teachers are cool, and the classrooms have everything."

If the foster system had taught her anything, it was to tell her temporary parents what they wanted to hear. Less trouble that way. And she hadn't totally lied. The school had the best facilities she had ever seen. Jaxon had studied in everything from run-down public schools in bad parts of town to small classes run by tutors at group homes, and now the most exclusive private school in Los Angeles.

The car pulled out into LA afternoon traffic. Isadore put on some classical music and set the volume low.

"This is Mozart's Symphony Number 40," she said. "It's good for you to learn about classical music. It helps the developing mind."

Jaxon looked out the window so her foster mother didn't see her roll her eyes. Isadore and Stephen were always saying stuff like that.

"So did you make any friends?" Isadore asked.

"I met a lot of people. There's a girl named Courtney who I think will be talking to me a lot."

"That's wonderful! I know you're going to be happy there. It's not easy to get a spot in that place. We got you in by the skin of our teeth."

Isadore didn't seem to need a response, so Jaxon didn't bother to say anything. She daydreamed as she looked beyond the snarled highway traffic, beyond LA's grim skyline, and wondered what Otto was doing right now. Would she ever see him again?

# Chapter 6

JUNE 5, 2016, OUTSKIRTS OF
SAN FRANCISCO, CALIFORNIA
8:25 AM

Otto Heike walked by the side of Inter-state 5, picking up trash and putting it in a large garbage bag. He and the rest of his crew wore identical orange jumpsuits with the word CONVICT written in large black letters on the chest and back. The prisoners hobbled along like old men thanks to their ankle chains, which clinked as they moved and made an odd counterpoint to the whoosh of traffic nearby. Two prison guards flanked them, holding rifles and staring at them from behind mirrored shades.

*So this is my future.* Otto bent to pick up a rotten old package of half-eaten fried chicken. Eighteen and already a convict. The judge had given him two years in prison for burning the greenhouse back at the group home, a crime he hadn't even committed. The judge said that now that Otto was eighteen, he could be tried as an adult, unlike for the other fires he had actually set when he was younger. It felt as though he was getting a delayed punishment for his real crimes. Otto fantasized about burning the courthouse down. It would serve them right.

At least the judge took pity on him and put him in a minimum-security prison. Otto didn't want to think about what would happen to him in some of California's tougher jails.

His parents had barely talked to him since he got locked up. In the month he'd been here, they hadn't come to any of the weekly visitors' days and had only called twice to chew him out and remind him how disappointed they were in him. As if he didn't know. They'd been telling him that since he was a kid.

An incoherent yell came from the highway as a car raced past—something that might have been, "Pick this up, lowlife!"—and a garbage bag flew out of the window. Otto leapt aside to avoid being hit, his ankle chains getting snarled around his legs and making him fall. The garbage bag burst against the gritty earth, spilling out old food and crushed beer cans and stuff Otto didn't even want to try and identify.

"On your feet and clean that up," one of the guards said with a wicked grin.

"Trash picking up trash," the other said.

Otto untangled himself and rose, dusting off his jumpsuit. Sometimes the guards harassed you if your clothes got dirty out here—took away rec time in the yard or made you eat your dinner in your cell. They were always thinking of some way to take it out on you. One of the guys, in jail for stealing cars, was missing two front teeth after some imagined infraction made one of the meaner guards lose his temper.

"I got to get out of here," Otto said under his breath for the millionth time that month.

"What you say, pyro?" one of the guards asked.

"I said 'I got a lot of trash here,' sir," Otto replied.

"Don't want any of your trash talking, kid," the second guard said. "Hey, Joe, get it? Trash talking! We got ourselves some talking trash!"

Both guards guffawed.

*Forget the courthouse,* Otto decided. *I want to burn down the prison.*

As Otto cleaned up the mess so kindly deposited by one of California's finer citizens, he wished for the thousandth time that he didn't have his urge.

He'd been lighting fires since he was a kid. It had started with small stuff that all kids did: igniting a pile of dry leaves with a box of stolen matches or melting one of his plastic army men to see what it would mutate into. While most kids did that once or twice and went on to other things, he had become obsessed. Fire was one of the most powerful forces in the world, and he could control it. All it took was one little spark and a bit of flammable material, and he could almost be like a god.

Soon piles of leaves and model soldiers weren't good enough. He graduated to piles of old schoolbooks and the mailbox of the crabby old woman across the street. He knew what he was doing was twisted, and that only made it more appealing. Every time his parents nagged him, every time he caught his dad stumbling in at three in the morning with some woman's lipstick on his cheek, every time something went wrong at school, there was always the flame waiting for him. It let him be in control again. Dr. Hollis made him realize that.

But before he had been caught, before he had gotten help, all he knew was that setting fires was the only thing that made him feel at the center of things. His parents sure as hell didn't do that. Dad was always who-knew-where, and Mom... well, if Mom was sober enough to walk in a straight line, that was only because it was still early in the day.

The neighbors' barn had been a turning point. It wasn't some random object that didn't affect anyone or something like Ms. Cronan's mailbox, which counted as a punishment for being such a mean person. This time it was downright cruel. Mr. and Mrs. Bunsen were a kind old couple who had never said a cross word to him. They had a barn in their backyard from the days when they were younger and kept horses. All those horses were dead by the time he was in elementary school, and the barn was sort of a memento for them.

The night it happened, he'd been in his room studying. Mom had been sitting downstairs, drinking in front of the TV, when Dad came home. There'd been a squawk from Mom and a sharp answer from Dad. Then they both started shouting at the same time, neither of them listening, neither of them stopping, and Otto knew it would go on all night. He'd been there before.

Otto had set down his pen and looked at his half-finished math homework. A distant, hollow feeling came over him, a feeling he knew well, yet far more powerful this time. He opened the top desk drawer, took out a pile of old notebooks, and found the Ziploc bag hidden beneath. In it were half a dozen lighters, a bunch of matches, and some fireworks he'd bought when they'd gone down to Hilton Head in South Carolina for summer vacation.

He grabbed a box of matches and put the bag away. One box was all he needed. Amazing what could come from such a little thing. Otto stuffed it in his pocket and put on his shoes. In that weird, detached calm he always got before he lit, he went downstairs and walked right by his parents, red-faced and standing two inches apart in the living room, screaming at each other and completely oblivious to his presence.

From the living room, Otto passed through the laundry room and opened a door into the garage. There, past Mom and Dad's cars, was the lawn mower and a jerry can of gasoline. He grabbed the can without breaking stride and walked out into the night.

He didn't remember much after that. There was the old musk of the barn interior, with its moldering bales of hay and dry wood walls and rafters. There was the splash of the gasoline and its sweet, sharp tang, and the rasp of a match. The next thing he remembered was the cop's gentle pressure on his neck as he ducked Otto's head to put him in the backseat of a police car.

Why did they always do that? They made sure you didn't bump your head as they took away your freedom. Otto supposed it was so they didn't get accused of police brutality. It seemed strange though, that little bit of care in a brutal system.

And now he was here, in an orange jumpsuit, picking up trash by the side of the highway.

He really, really needed to light.

The squeal of tires made Otto flinch and look up, wary of another bit of trash getting launched at him at sixty miles an hour. A red Subaru Impreza screeched to a halt on the shoulder, its tires spitting gravel. The convicts stopped what they were doing and stared. The two guards swiveled and raised their rifles halfway, unsure of what to do.

A gorgeous blond woman in a miniskirt and halter top emerged from the driver's seat. Every man, both prisoner and guard, was too busy staring at her cleavage to notice what she held in her hands.

"Hello, boys."

The men gaped.

She jerked her arms. Something small and black flew at both guards. There was a boom and a flash, then a sharp hiss. Otto's eyes widened at the lovely flame.

It was gone too quick, replaced by thick smoke. The guards choked and staggered back. Within seconds, they had fallen and lay on the ground, racked with coughs.

A strong hand grabbed his wrist. Otto turned to face a thirty-something man with a slight build and intense eyes fixed on him from behind a pair of glasses. He looked like some science geek, but he carried himself like a soldier.

"Get in the car," the stranger demanded.

"But... I..."

"We need you to help Jaxon. She's in danger."

"Jaxon? Is she here? I can't break out of prison!"

The man slapped Otto across the face. "You have no future. Your parents don't give a damn about you. The system doesn't give a damn about you. Want a future? Get in the car."

Without waiting for an answer, the man dragged Otto toward the Subaru. The ankle chains slowed Otto down, and he stumbled as he tried to keep up. He didn't know why he was following, but something in the stranger's words hit him deep. There was nothing for him here.

"Wait! Take me!" one of the convicts shouted.

"Me too!" another cried.

The whole crowd of prisoners shuffled forward, their ankle chains clanking. The woman who had thrown the bombs ducked down and signaled to someone inside the car.

A moment later, the passenger-side door opened. A huge man dressed in black with a tribal tattoo on the right half of his face and a shaved scalp stood and leveled an assault rifle on the approaching crowd.

The convicts stopped. The stranger dragging Otto toward the car kept on going. The woman with the bombs flung open the back door. The man holding Otto put a hand on the back of Otto's head and pushed him down into the backseat like a cop putting a prisoner in the back of a squad car

Otto landed on the seat hard. The stranger sat beside him and slammed the door shut. A moment later, Otto jerked back as the woman hit the gas and the car shot down the highway.

"Where are you taking me?" Otto shouted.

"Shut up, we're not out yet," the guy who had grabbed him said, pushing his glasses back onto the bridge of his nose just before they slipped off. He pulled a semi-automatic pistol from his jacket pocket and looked out the rear windshield. "We got company!"

Otto had the weird thought that whoever this guy was, he had seen too many action movies.

The wail of a police siren made Otto turn and look out the rear window. "That's the second squad car! They're with the other work crew."

"They should have stayed with them," the woman driving said.

"Want me to get them?" the hulking monster with the assault rifle asked.

"No, I can handle this," the driver replied.

The big guy looked disappointed.

The woman flicked open a panel on the dashboard and revealed a row of red buttons. She wiggled her fingers along the row as if she couldn't decide which one to press then jabbed her forefinger at one.

Otto heard a soft clunk from the rear of the car. An instant later, there was a boom and a flash that almost blinded Otto even though he wasn't looking out the back window. He glanced back. The police car was swerving off the highway from a billowing cloud of green smoke. The vehicle crunched into the shoulder and came to a stop in a cloud of dust. In a minute, it had receded out of sight.

"We got him!" the man who had pulled him into the car said. "We're in the clear."

Once again, Otto felt as if the guy was fantasizing he was in an action movie. But wait—flash bombs, a police chase, explosives that popped out of the back of a car at the touch of a button... they really were in an action movie!

"What the hell is going on?" Otto demanded.

The woman driving looked at him in the rearview mirror. "You just sit tight there, honey. Everything's going to be okay."

"Okay? You just busted me out of prison! If I get caught, it'll be another five years at least."

"You ain't gonna get caught," the burly man in the passenger's seat said. "Push your legs between the seats here so I can get those chains off."

Otto did as he was told. The man produced a small leather case from his pocket and opened it to reveal several metal tools with curved ends.

"Are those lockpicks?" Otto asked.

"Your dossier says you're smart," the man said, "but we won't be using those." He picked out what looked like a key from the collection. "Handcuff key." He stuck the key into the lock on Otto's ankle.

"My dossier?" Otto asked.

The metal band around his right ankle popped open, and the man started on the other one.

Otto took a deep breath and looked around. They were on a lonely stretch of highway with no one in sight. "Okay, so tell me what's going on."

The man in the backseat with him adjusted his glasses. "A secret government agency called the Poseidon Project is after Jaxon because of her special powers. They want to make her a slave."

"Special powers?" Otto tried to play dumb, but his curiosity got the better of him. "Wait, how did you know about that?"

The man's face turned grim. "Because I used to work for that agency. I quit when I realized what they were up to, and now I'm fighting them. My name's James Yuhle. Sorry for slapping you."

"Um, no problem. So what's with Jaxon anyway? Is she some kind of mutant?"

Yuhle laughed. "A mutant? No. She's descended from the Atlanteans."

"What? You mean Atlantis? The sunken continent? That's a myth."

"Maybe, maybe not. The Atlanteans are real though. Didn't you notice she looks different, like a mix of all races at once?"

"Yeah, she's mixed race, so what?"

Yuhle shook his head. "She isn't mixed race. She's a different race, a different species, perhaps. She isn't human."

"Oh, come off it!"

"Can normal teenage girls beat up half a dozen soldiers?"

"I helped," Otto said, feeling a bit put out.

The burly guy in the front laughed. "Don't get jealous of your little girlfriend, buddy. Give her some training, and she could flatten me too."

"Or maybe without training," the woman driving the car said, giving him a teasing smile.

"Not a chance," the big man said.

Otto looked at the mass of muscle in front of him and wondered.

The car pulled to a stop at the side of the highway, right behind another Subaru of a different make and color. There was no one inside.

"Let's go," the driver said, looking around, probably to see if there were any other cars in sight.

They got out of the car and into the other one. As they pulled away, the car they had been in erupted in flames. Otto looked back in awe before forcing himself to turn around.

"Covering our tracks," the driver said, smiling at him in the rearview mirror.

They drove in silence for a time. Otto felt overwhelmed. He had resigned himself to being stuck in prison, and now he was on a remote highway headed east with a group of heavily armed strangers.

At last he found the courage to speak. "So where are we going?"

"The Mojave desert in Nevada," the driver replied. "I'm Vivian, by the way, and this lump of barely restrained violence next to me is Grunt."

Otto raised an eyebrow. "Grunt?"

The big, bald man turned to face Otto. His tribal tattoo rippled as he moved his head. "It's a nickname I got in one of the wars. It's the only name you need to know."

Otto shifted in his seat. "Um... right. So did you two break out of that government project too?"

"The Poseidon Project?" Yuhle said with a laugh. "No, they're mercenaries."

"Fighting for the right cause for once," Grunt mumbled, looking back out the window at the passing desert.

"We're called the Atlantis Allegiance," Vivian explained. "We have a secret base in the desert. It's near the site where the government tested the early atomic bombs, starting in the fifties. Yuhle likes the symbolism. We like the fact that there are no neighbors for twenty miles."

"The Atlantis Allegiance?" Otto asked. "What are you, hippies or something?"

Grunt turned in his seat again. "Do I look like a hippie to you, pyro?"

Otto gulped and managed to squeak out, "No."

Yuhle leaned over to Otto. "Don't mind Grunt. He's a little touchy about pretty much everything."

"So what does Atlantis got to do with all this?" Otto asked.

Yuhle adjusted his glasses. "It's a long story, but as luck would have it, we have a long ride ahead of us. So you just sit back and get comfortable."

Otto looked out the window as the desert rolled by. Yeah, get comfortable.

He had a feeling he wouldn't be comfortable for a long, long time.

# Chapter 7

JUNE 5, 2016, LOS ANGELES,
CALIFORNIA

9:15 AM

"Concentrate."

Jaxon and her martial arts instructor, Marquis, stood in the Grants' exercise room. Both wore traditional training uniforms—a white cotton top similar to a karate uniform and a pair of black cotton pants. For her first lesson, Marquis had laid padded mats over the central part of the room. Around them was a variety of weights, exercise equipment, a punching bag, and racks of weird weapons Jaxon hadn't seen outside of a movie. A large window looked out over the Grants' backyard and her foster father's greenhouse. Despite Stephen Grant's invitation to visit his personal botanical laboratory, she hadn't been taken in there yet.

"Your foster parents told me you're pretty fit," Marquis said. He was a lean man in his mid-thirties, with dark features and heavy black eyebrows. "Strength and speed are important, but even more important is concentration and technique. Aikido will teach you how to channel your energy. When a young girl finds herself in danger, it's usually against a grown man who is much bigger and stronger than she is. Aikido will teach you how to defeat him using his own size and strength."

*Or I can just snap his wrist like a twig,* Jaxon replied silently.

The instructor continued. "Aikido is a Japanese martial art. While it was developed in the twentieth century, its roots go back to ancient times. The word can be translated as 'the way of harmonious spirit.' By practicing the channeling of external energy, you also align your internal energy. I don't mind telling you Aikido's brought me a lot of inner peace.

I was pretty messed up when I was your age—just ask the LAPD." Marquis grinned.

"So this is, like, meditation or something?" Jaxon asked.

"You can think of it as moving meditation. It's also a nonviolent means of self-defense."

"How can self-defense be nonviolent?"

"By defeating your opponent with his own violent energy. You don't turn that violent energy into violence but into a trap. Aikido has a number of techniques like flips, wrist locks, and dodges. First let me demonstrate, then I'll show you some techniques you can practice. Ready? Throw me to the floor. If you can't do that, try to stop me from moving. If you can't do that, just try to hold on to me."

Jaxon snorted. This guy didn't know what he was up against. *Careful you don't hurt him. He's a nice enough guy, if a bit cocky.*

Without warning, Jaxon lunged forward. She meant to grab his shoulders, spin him around, and toss him to the mat.

That didn't happen.

He wasn't in front of her anymore. In a flash and a blur, he was beside and a little behind her.

Jaxon spun around and tried to grab him again. This time he didn't even bother to move his feet. He simply twisted his upper body in a confusing way that dazzled Jaxon's vision. One of her hands missed him completely. The other briefly touched his arm before he slipped out of her grasp.

Jaxon made another swipe and didn't even connect.

"You seem to be going for my arm," Marquis said. "Very well, here you go."

He stuck his arm forward, elbow bent so his forearm was between him and her, as if he was some gentleman in a historical movie, offering his arm to the lady of the manor so they could walk through the garden.

*That's totally a trap.* Jaxon pretended to go for the arm he offered and instead reached below it to grab at his belt.

It was gone before her fingertips made it within an inch. Marquis was behind her again. Jaxon growled in frustration.

"Okay, let's try again," he said. "Now I'll let you grab both my shoulders. Don't worry, I won't hurt you. Aikido isn't about hurting your opponent, it's about neutralizing him."

Marquis stood motionless in front of her. Warily, Jaxon put her hands on his shoulders. She had to reach up a bit because he was a full six feet tall and she was only five feet three. He probably underestimated her because she was short. Lots of people did that. Out of frustration, she gripped a little harder than she needed to.

Marquis should have let out a yelp of pain. He should have writhed and struggled. Instead he gyrated in what could only be described as some sort of arcane dance move. Jaxon felt her grip slip away.

Her Aikido instructor stayed close, letting Jaxon try to get a hold of him, but no matter what she did, she couldn't get a decent grip. It was like wrestling with an empty shirt.

Jaxon felt her frustration growing. She always avoided fights, and now that she was in one, her opponent was making a fool of her. Sure, he kept a calm face, but she would bet a million bucks he was laughing on the inside.

Gritting her teeth, she renewed her efforts. She swung at him, tried to grapple, forgetting, in her anger, to hold back her strength and speed. The two fighters danced around the mat in a blur, moving more by sense than sight.

After a minute, Jaxon realized she wasn't even touching him anymore.

"Damn it!" she shouted.

She stomped off the mat and gave the punching bag a hard right hook that sent it swinging high enough to slap the ceiling. Jaxon didn't see that. She was already leaving the room.

Isadore blocked the exit. She frowned at her foster daughter, arms folded. "Marquis was very difficult to hire. He's in high demand. You're not going to waste your lesson, are you?"

"He's not teaching me anything!"

"That's because you're not paying attention. Go back and finish your lesson."

Jaxon growled and almost shoved past Isadore. At the last moment, Jaxon controlled herself. She didn't want to get kicked out of yet another foster home in her first week. She had a good thing here—her own room, an amazing mansion to live in, and all sorts of private lessons. The Grants seemed eager to give her plenty of education. If she got kicked out, who knew where she'd end up? Maybe some run-down place where they only wanted her for the money the state gave out, or the home of some pervert.

So she had no choice but to buck up and face the situation. When did she ever have a choice? Jaxon growled, turned, and walked back to the mat. The punching bag was still swinging, almost touching the ceiling. Jaxon glanced at it. The thing weighed fifty pounds at least. She had to hide her abilities better or she would be singled out again.

Marquis smiled at her. He didn't seem to have noticed the punching bag. That struck her as odd, but she was too angry to think about it.

"Ready to try again?" he asked.

"Whatever."

"Now this time, try to keep your emotions in check. You don't want to get mad in a fight. Anger will cloud your judgment and make you lose. Anger is what gets people into fights in the first place, so that is their first mistake. Fear will do the same since they are so often linked. Keep your mind clear and detached from what you are doing."

*Skip the Yoda crap and let's fight, okay?*

"Ready?" Marquis asked.

"Whatever."

Jaxon approached more carefully this time, knowing Marquis wouldn't be as easy to hit as those soldiers in the greenhouse. Thinking of them, she decided it might not be a bad idea to pick up some tips. They might prove useful if those guys come back. Marquis was right. She should try to calm herself and learn something.

She feinted to the left then shot to the right and tried to grab the front of his shirt. To her surprise, she actually managed to. A moment later, she realized he had let her. She was flung around, lost her footing, and would have fallen if Marquis hadn't caught her and, spinning her again, made her pirouette a good five feet away.

Without missing a beat, she dove for his legs. This time she was scooped up off her feet and set down. Before she could make a move, Marquis had backed off.

Grinding her teeth, Jaxon lunged and grabbed for him again.

It was the same as their first fight. He dodged this way and that, faster than even her incredible reflexes could follow. Her fingers grasped empty air or barely brushed the fabric of his uniform.

"Bit like life's problems, isn't it?" Marquis said as he bobbed just out of reach. He was grinning, and that made Jaxon even angrier. "You wrestle with them, you scream at them, and the solution always eludes you. And that's because"—he grabbed her and flipped her—"if you charge at them like a raging bull, they'll end up defeating you."

Jaxon was flat on her back, yet she hadn't felt a thing. He hadn't thrown her to the mat; he had *placed* her there.

Okay, she definitely needed to learn from this guy. But first, she needed to put him in his place.

She sprang to her feet and launched herself at him. Of course he wasn't there once she made it.

Suddenly she couldn't move her arm. Marquis had her in a wrist-and-arm lock, pushing her hand down and her elbow the wrong way. Jaxon stared, bewildered. It didn't hurt at all, but she couldn't move.

Gritting her teeth, she put more energy into her arm. Slowly, her wrist and elbow began to bend.

Marquis looked impressed. "You're very strong."

"You don't know the half of it."

"Unfortunately, you can't solve life's problems through brute strength."

Jaxon found herself on her back once again. This time she didn't get up. She didn't see much point.

Marquis put his hands on his hips and looked down at her. "Are you quitting on me?"

"I'm not a quitter," Jaxon growled. "If I was a quitter, I would have slashed my wrists years ago."

Marquis frowned. "Don't talk about suicide. You're sixteen years old. I know people dying of AIDS who still cling to life, knowing that it's precious. Life is the most valuable gift we're ever given. It's not something to be thrown away."

"Don't worry, I wouldn't off myself. Faced with someone as annoying as you, it's tempting though. Then at least you'd leave me in peace."

"Don't turn into an emo. I thought that group was out of fashion."

"You should visit my new school. I'll show you worse."

Marquis extended his hand.

"I'm not falling for that," Jaxon said.

"It's good to be suspicious of your opponent's motives. Don't worry though. I'm just offering to help you up."

"I can help myself," Jaxon said, getting to her feet.

"That's what these lessons are supposed to teach you. Shall we try again?"

Jaxon shrugged. "What for? You'll only throw me down again."

"That's because you'll try to solve the same problem the same way, and since it didn't work the last several times, it won't work again. Let me show you some techniques that will work."

For the next two hours, Marquis took her through several basic moves. He showed her the proper stance to lower her center of gravity and make it harder for someone to knock her down. He showed her various blocks using her arms and legs, and he demonstrated them by attacking her slowly while telling her what he was going to do. Once she got the hang of it, he increased his speed. Soon he stopped telling her how he was going to attack. Jaxon's abnormally fast reactions meant she could easily stop him, but she saw that the techniques of Aikido made her blocks easier and more effective.

They also kept her from snapping Marquis's wrists. He may be annoying, but only perverts deserved that.

As the afternoon's lesson continued, Jaxon found herself growing calmer. The movements Marquis was teaching her really were like a moving meditation. Plus they were useful. The threat of those mysterious men in the greenhouse still troubled her. She needed to take in all this martial arts stuff for if—no, *when*—they found her again.

In the meantime, she was really enjoying it. She had always hated sports class because the other girls would make fun of her for being short or weird-looking or whatever, and she was always picked last even though she wasn't the worst player. This was different though. Putting a ball through a basket was just a game. Learning how to block an attacker's punch could be a lifesaver.

And Jaxon had a feeling she'd put these lessons into practice sooner rather than later.

# Chapter 8

JUNE 5, 2016, MOJAVE DESERT, NEVADA

6:30 PM

Otto woke up when the car stopped. The excitement of his prison break and the tension of the long car ride with a crowd of heavily armed strangers had exhausted him, and he had drifted off to sleep. He didn't know how many miles of desert had passed by as his body and mind took a break.

Now the sky was reddening to the west, and he found himself in a barren stretch of desert. The car had stopped at the end of a dirt road in front of a gate and a chain-link fence topped by razor wire. Beyond were a couple of prefab homes and some trailers. Four Rottweilers stood behind the fence, barking their heads off.

"Welcome to your new home," Yuhle said from the seat next to him. The scientist adjusted his glasses and gave Otto a triumphant smile. He'd stowed his pistol, which was just fine by Otto. He suspected Yuhle didn't really know how to use it and might shoot his foot off.

"Where are we?" Otto asked, rubbing his eyes.

"The middle of nowhere, honey," Vivian said from the driver's seat. "No night-clubs, no bars, no cinemas, no shopping malls... I call it Boringville."

"War is weeks of grinding boredom punctuated by moments of sheer terror," Grunt said, stepping out of the car. He flung out his arms and ran to the gate. "My babies! Did you miss me?"

The Rottweilers wagged their tails and jumped up on the fence, making it shake to its foundations. Grunt punched a key code into a panel by the side of the gate. With a low hum from a hidden motor, the gate slowly slid open. The Rottweilers ran out and leapt on Grunt, licking his face and hands.

"Oh, I missed you so much!" Grunt cooed as he petted them.

Otto got out of the car and walked toward the dogs. The Rottweilers spotted him, snarled, and charged

"Yikes!" Otto cried, hurrying back toward the car.

"Heel!" Grunt shouted.

The Rottweilers stopped as if they'd slammed into an invisible wall. They immediately sat on their haunches and glared at Otto, licking their chops.

"Don't worry," the mercenary said. "They're just not used to you."

Vivian drove the car through the gate, leaving Otto stranded in the driveway with the dogs and Grunt.

"Um, you sure they're not going to eat me?" Otto asked.

Grunt gave him a wicked grin. "Not unless I tell them to. This here is War, this little darling's name is Famine, she's Pestilence, and the last one is Death. I named them after the Four Horsemen of the Apocalypse."

"How charming." Otto made a wide circle around them and slipped through the gate as a menacing growl emerged from four canine throats.

The car had shot forward in a cloud of dust and grit and been parked by a few other vehicles—three cars, a van with no windows, and a Humvee. No one else was in sight, but he noticed security cameras posted in strategic locations around the compound, covering every approach. The little cluster of buildings stood on a low rise, offering a good view of the surrounding desert. Otto looked back the way he had come and saw that the dirt path ran for almost a mile before becoming a gravel road leading off toward the horizon.

As he thumbed in the key code to lock the gate again, Grunt said, "We're in the middle of nowhere. Our nearest neighbors are five miles away. A group of survivalists. I've checked on them, and I'm sure they've checked on us. They won't be any trouble. A little beyond that is some religious nut job family. One man and I don't know how many wives, plus a whole mess of kids. All that guy wants is to be left alone to rule his little version of paradise. He won't be any trouble either."

Ordering the dogs to stay, Grunt followed Otto toward the buildings where Yuhle and Vivian waited for them.

"So now what?" Otto asked once they'd joined up with them.

Yuhle shrugged. "Not much. Just save your girlfriend, defeat a maverick general, elude the Pentagon and CIA, and reunite the lost citizens of Atlantis."

Otto laughed. It all sounded so ridiculous. "The four of us are going to do all that?"

"Five. You haven't met Edward yet," Vivian said.

"Yeah, the four of us and a guy named Edward," Otto muttered, shaking his head. He was beginning to think he had been kidnapped by lunatics. Maybe he should run off and take his chances with the religious nut jobs.

"Don't underestimate Edward. It's easy, but don't do it," Yuhle said. "Now for some ground rules. You have that small trailer over there for your own use. You'll find sheets, toiletries, everything you need. I'll go into town later and buy you some clothes. I figure you probably don't want to go around in your prison uniform for the rest of your life. No leaving the compound. No making calls, not that you have a phone anyway. We have satellite Internet, but that's monitored by Edward, so you'll have to get his say-so to use it. No emails."

"Sounds like I'm still in prison," Otto said.

"Except you won't get victimized by axe murderers," Yuhle said. "Plus you get to fight for freedom. Feel free to make a break for it if you want. Assuming you can outrun the Four Rottweilers of the Apocalypse and make it through a hundred miles of America's worst desert, all you'll find at the other end is a wanted poster with your face on it. But don't worry, you won't be bored here. Grunt and Vivian are starting your training tomorrow."

"Training?"

Vivian smiled. "Explosives, firearms, camouflage—you'll like it."

Otto shook his head. "I don't understand any of this."

"You will, honey," Vivian said, putting a hand on his shoulder. "It's a lot to absorb. The first thing to understand is that the world isn't like you think it is.

All those conspiracy theories and legends you've read about or seen on TV? Half of them are true, and the other half are just propaganda put there to make you blind to the truth. Edward can explain it better than me though. Let me take you to see him."

"I got to stow the ordnance," Grunt said.

"I'll help you," Yuhle replied, walking beside the mercenary and trying to imitate his swagger.

As the two men walked off, Vivian led Otto to the larger of the two mobile homes. Otto noticed an oversized satellite dish and several antennae on the roof.

Vivian opened the door and ushered Otto into the dark interior. The windows were all covered with black cloth, and the only light came from a host of computer screens that nearly surrounded a dark figure hunched over one of several keyboards. The stale, musty odor of unwashed bodies and old socks assailed his nostrils. In the background, Otto heard a man speaking in Spanish over the radio, faint and barely audible over the static. He sounded scared, earnest, as if he only had a few minutes to say the most important thing in the world.

An office chair creaked as it turned. In the glow of the computer screens, Otto saw the disheveled figure of a man in his twenties. His clothes were wrinkled and a size too big, even for his overweight body. His T-shirt was on inside out. Bloodshot eyes studied Otto from above several days' growth of beard.

"Hey, pyro!" the man said in a friendly manner.

"Why does everyone call me that?" Otto griped.

"Because that's what you are. You can call me Nerdy Computer Guy if you want, or you can call me Edward."

"How about I call you Edward and you call me Otto?"

"Sure enough, pyro—I mean, Otto."

"Behave, Edward," Vivian said then turned to Otto. "You'll have to forgive him, honey. He's not very well socialized. He knows more about this stuff than anyone though."

"Knows more about what?" Otto asked.

Edward looked eager. "About what's really going on! What they don't tell us in the newspapers. What even most government officials don't know."

"Like what?"

"Like everything! Who's really in charge. Humanity's real history. What's been suppressed and twisted so we'd be a flock of sheep doing whatever they want."

"Ah... right." Was this guy a nut or something? And why were a pair of mercenaries and some gun-toting scientist hanging out with him? Otto looked past Edward's shoulder at the computer screens. One showed a mass of text. Another had a video of what looked like a protest in the Middle East. The third had a blueprint of some building.

Edward pointed at Otto. "I see you don't believe me. A common reaction from the sheeple."

"Sheeple?"

"Sheep people. It's what they want us to be." Edward spun around on his office chair, went too far and banged his knee against the table, cursed under his breath, and righted his chair. "Look at this."

He clicked away at his keyboard. Some images came up on a large screen in front of him. He spread out his hands to two other keyboards flanking the first and typed on both at the same time. Otto raised his eyebrow in appreciation.

A flurry of images came up on the three screens. Otto saw fuzzy images of disc- and cigar-shaped UFOs. Most looked as if they were high in the atmosphere. In a couple of shots, they buzzed over what looked like military bases.

"You believe in these things?" Otto asked.

"The government does," Edward said, bringing up more images.

Otto leaned in and studied the images. They didn't look all that impressive. "Photoshop." He shrugged.

Edward waggled a finger. "Ah, that's the usual reaction, and in many cases you'd be right. The Internet is filled with faked photos of everything from celebrity boob jobs to the Abominable Snowman. But these are real."

"How can you tell?"

"I'm a computer genius, in case my fashion sense didn't clue you in, and why would the government fake UFO photos in top-secret documents?"

Otto snorted. "These are secret government files?"

"Hacked them myself."

Otto turned to Vivian, who nodded.

"He's one of the best computer hackers in the country, honey—"

"The world!" Edward corrected.

"And he's gotten into files of government agencies you and your congressman have never heard of."

Otto cocked his head. "Wait, no way. So UFOs are real?" He read the text around the images and saw all sorts of government jargon, along with mathematical formulae he couldn't even begin to understand.

"That's not the only thing that's real, pyro—I mean, Otto," Edward said. "Ever hear of the Roswell UFO crash? Real. CIA conspiracy to kill JFK? Real. The Soviet Union developing a weather machine? Real. Loch Ness Monster? Bunch of drunken Scotsmen seeing things and hoping to cash in on the tourist industry. Moon landings? Faked."

"The moon landings weren't faked," Otto objected. "My science teacher taught us how all those conspiracy websites are wrong. Like they say the flag wouldn't be waving because there's no air to move it. My teacher said that because there's no air, there's no friction, so when the astronauts planted the flag and straightened it out, it kept moving for a while because of inertia."

Edward laughed. "Those conspiracy websites are fronts for the government. They deliberately make bad arguments so smart people will debunk them. That way only really stupid people believe in the conspiracy, while anyone with brains thinks we really did go to the moon. If the government is going to fake a moon landing, don't you think they're going to do a proper job?"

"So we didn't go to the moon in 1969?"

"No, we went to the moon in 1957, or '58. That's a matter of debate."

"So we did go to the moon?"

"Yeah, using reverse-engineered technology from the crashed UFO at Roswell.

But if the government had admitted it then, the Soviets would have known we'd gotten our hands on alien technology. No way we could have gotten to the moon so early otherwise. So we waited until 1969, made a big show of a space race, forced the Soviets to throw heaps of money at their own space program, and faked the landings."

"Why not just go back?" *Was this guy for real?*

Edward shrugged. "Why spend the money? There's nothing up there except a few archaeological sites, but that's another story. Besides, the real moon lander looked too alien. We needed a fake lander that looked like something made by a government committee."

Otto sighed and rubbed his temples. At least he didn't have to share a trailer with this guy.

The Spanish voice on the radio increased in pitch. He sounded panicked and spoke quickly, as if he didn't have much time. Edward turned and stared at the large shortwave transmitter and receiver on the next table.

There was a crash in the background on the radio. The voice screamed, cut short by a burst of noise that sounded like gunshots. Then silence. After a moment, the transmission cut off, leaving only dead air.

Edward bowed his head. "Another freedom fighter gone." He sighed.

"Did you... know him?" Otto asked.

For a moment, Edward didn't answer. At last he looked up with tears in his eyes. "Know him? No. Just another champion of the truth. He's been broadcasting on and off for a couple of years now. I triangulated his position a few times and found he was in El Salvador. He kept moving around, but it looks like they finally caught up with him."

"Who?"

Edward shrugged. "CIA, KGB, Mossad, who knows? Probably not our enemies though. He never spoke about Atlantis."

"Yuhle mentioned Atlantis. You're not going to tell me that Atlantis was real too, are you?"

Edward gave the shortwave radio a final mournful look before swiveling his chair to face Otto. "We're still trying to figure out if there was actually a continent that sank in ancient times. The Atlanteans are real though."

"More of your aliens?"

"No, they're human. Beyond human, in a way. They have special powers, like super strength and speed and individual powers like, oh, I don't know, making plants grow unusually fast."

Otto stepped back. "How do you know about that?"

"It's our business to know. And of course we're not the only ones. We need to get your Atlantean girlfriend out of their clutches before she ends up like that guy on the radio."

Otto hurried out of the building, almost tripping over Vivian's legs. He needed some air. His stomach felt shaky, and he was sure he would puke soon.

He was greeted by a magnificent sunset. The entire western sky looked as if it were on fire. Low, stripy clouds had been painted a deep red that blended well with the rosy glow of the sky. He stopped and gaped. He remembered a vacation to Arizona he had taken with his parents when he was a kid, and how those desert sunsets had entranced him. They entranced him even more now. Yeah, the whole sky was one fire. Imagine that...

A low growl made him jump.

"Easy, Famine," Grunt's voice said.

Otto looked around and saw the mercenary standing a few yards away, smoking a cigarette. The red glow at the cigarette's end as he inhaled caught Otto's attention. Grunt had an automatic pistol and a Bowie knife strapped to his belt. Otto suspected he never went anywhere without them. One of his Rottweilers lay at his feet.

"Come on over. She won't bite as long as I'm around."

Otto walked over to him.

"Hell of a sunset, eh?" Grunt said.

"Yeah," Otto whispered, looking at the horizon again.

"Looks like one big fire, doesn't it?"

Otto nodded. It was exactly what he'd been thinking.

Grunt finished his cigarette, dropped it on the ground, and crushed it with the heel of his boot. Then he fished out another from his pack and lit it with a

Zippo lighter. The flame shot up a full six inches. Apparently Grunt was one of those people who put his lighter at maximum to look cool. Probably used it as a weapon too.

Otto glanced at the bright flame dancing in the evening breeze.

Grunt raised the lighter. Otto's eyes followed. Grunt passed the Zippo back and forth in front of Otto's face.

"Pretty, isn't it?"

Otto didn't know what to say, but he had to agree. So pretty.

Grunt snapped the Zippo shut, making Otto start.

"You're weak," Grunt said. "Man up, kid. Weak people get killed in missions like this." With that, the mercenary turned on his heel and stalked away, his dog trotting behind him.

# Chapter 9

JUNE 6, 2016, LOS ANGELES,
CALIFORNIA

6:30 AM

It was way, way too early. The Grants had woken Jaxon at five thirty. After some yoga stretches with Isadore, Stephen had made them a breakfast of muesli, homemade yogurt, and fruit. This was way different than Jaxon's usual pattern of stumbling out of bed as late as she could get away with and wolfing down some muffins and chocolate cereal. That wouldn't happen in this house.

"A healthy body for a healthy mind," Stephen had said. Whatever that meant.

Now she was sitting on a yoga mat in the exercise room, right by the rear window. Morning sunlight streamed in on the face of Juliette, her yoga and meditation teacher. She ran a studio that Isadore attended, and she had been hired by her foster mother to come give Jaxon private lessons. Stephen and Isadore were sparing no expense on what they thought Jaxon's education should be. Jaxon would have preferred if they saved their money and let her sleep in a bit. It was a school day, after all. Didn't she have enough to contend with?

Juliette was a thin woman in her forties with deep smile lines on her freckled face. Her straw-colored hair was pulled back in a ponytail, and she wore a leotard like Jaxon. She sat facing Jaxon in something called the lotus position, her legs crossed and the top of each foot resting on her opposite thigh. Juliette said it helped with stability and breathing, but Jaxon thought it made her look like a pretzel. Jaxon just sat with her legs crossed the normal way, wondering how her teacher could be at all comfortable.

"Now, Jaxon, we're going to start with some basic breathing exercises and guided meditation. This will help you relieve stress and control anger. Your foster mother says you've been through a lot, and meditation will help you get through it more easily."

Jaxon resisted the urge to roll her eyes. If Juliette wanted to help, she could find out who was after her and why. Then Juliette could find Jaxon's birth parents, make the kids at school stop bothering her, and about a million other things that needed fixing.

Breathing wasn't going to fix any of those things.

"First, sit up straight. Yes, I know you've heard that a lot. For meditation, it actually helps. Good posture helps with attitude too. It makes you feel optimistic. When you're walking, don't look down all the time—look straight ahead. A depressed posture encourages a depressed mind. Everything is connected, so working on one aspect of your being will help the others. Ignoring any aspect of your being will hurt the rest."

*Like trying to ignore that I'm not like anyone else in the world?*

Juliette continued. "Now close your eyes. To deal with the inner self, at first it's best to cut out the external world. I bet that's tempting for you sometimes. Closing your eyes cuts off one of the senses immediately. Sitting in a quiet place with no interruptions helps too. Now about what I was saying about each aspect of your character, plus the mind/body connection—we can't be whole persons if we don't accept our whole selves. There's a quote I read in the Gnostic Gospels that really resonated with me. 'If you let what is inside of you out of you, what is inside of you will save you. If you don't let what is inside of you out of you, what is inside of you will kill you.'"

Jaxon shuddered. That hit a bit too close to home.

Juliette's calm voice flowed on. "Now try breathing slowly and deeply from your diaphragm, in through your nose and out through your mouth. Steadily. Calmly. Deeply. Try to empty your mind."

Jaxon did as she was told, except for the emptying her mind part. She was still thinking of that quote Juliette had mentioned. Hiding her true nature had eaten her up all Jaxon's life. Maybe it wasn't so much that other people treated her as different; maybe her thinking of herself as different caused people to follow her lead. Why should she expect people to accept her when she didn't accept herself?

But what was the alternative? Embrace the fact that she had super-human powers? Accept that she was all alone in the world with no family and no heritage? How the hell could that help? Being different was dangerous. Those guys in the greenhouse had proved that. It was easy to say you had to let your true nature shine through, but what if your true nature made everyone scared of you?

Jaxon had enough rejection in her life as it was. There were enough people looking down on her. Even so, there was no need for her to be one of them.

Juliette was still talking. Her words ran over Jaxon's tumultuous mind without registering. Her soft tone and calm manner worked on Jaxon's mood, however, like massaging fingers easing her inner tension. Slowly, without her fully realizing it, her muscles relaxed and her thoughts moved more slowly. Yes, she did need to accept herself, and yes, that would be a long, hard fight. It could happen though. She just needed to accept her situation. Maybe there was some peace for her out there somewhere. No, that was the wrong way to put it. There *was* peace for her, and it was inside herself.

Finding it was the tricky part. She'd been criticizing herself as harshly as any of the endless series of bullies in her life. And unlike the bullies, she couldn't avoid herself.

Jaxon breathed more deeply, her mind emptying as Juliette's voice whispered in her ears. She didn't even focus on the words, just the soothing tone. Was she going to get this every morning? She hoped so.

Isadore's voice cut through the soft blanket of calm that enveloped her. "Jaxon! Time to get ready for school!"

So much for the relaxation. Jaxon sighed, thanked Juliette, and hurried to her room.

Isadore drove her, as usual. Stephen was usually in the greenhouse by the time she was ready for school. Jaxon was beginning to get curious about the greenhouse. As much as he talked about it, she still hadn't gotten in there.

"So how do you like Juliette?" her foster mother asked.

"She's cool."

"Could you elaborate?"

"Huh?"

"Do you like the meditation? Do you like what she says?" Isadore asked.

"Yeah, I guess." She didn't want to share her thoughts with her foster mother. Jaxon could barely process them herself, so she certainly wasn't going to talk about them with a stranger. She had made that mistake far too many times. Curious, she turned to her foster mother. "Why are you getting me so many tutors? I mean, I appreciate it and all, it just seems a bit much."

"We care about your education. We want you to learn how to control your anger and channel it into more productive avenues. We think you have a great future."

"As what?" Jaxon didn't think about the future much. She'd never really considered that she had one that wasn't more of the same. It wasn't as if she would become an adult and suddenly magically fit in.

"Just focus on your lessons for now, and we'll talk about that later. Oh, I had a talk with your new teacher, Mrs. Endersby, and she had a talk with the principal..."

Jaxon perked up. That didn't sound good.

"And we've decided to enroll you in summer school."

*"What?"*

"Now I know that doesn't sound like a whole lot of fun, but Mrs. Endersby thinks it's for the best. With all of your shuffling around between foster parents and group homes, you've missed a lot of classes. Your education has suffered."

Jaxon groaned and looked out the window. She knew this new foster home was too good to be true. Stephen and Isadore wanted to work her like a slave.

Her foster mother continued. "Think of it as an opportunity. You can catch up on your work and meet more people. It's so late in the year that if you don't go to summer school, you'd only be at this new school for a couple of weeks before summer vacation. This way you can get to know your classmates better."

"Yeah. That sounds wonderful."

"Sarcasm doesn't befit someone of your intelligence. Don't you want to make some friends?"

Jaxon didn't reply. Isadore wasn't going to listen to her anyway. Like all foster parents, she had an idea in her head of how she was going to mold her foster child in her own image. She thought that throwing money at the problem would make Jaxon fit in.

Yeah, right. Tell that to Courtney and her little flock of hangers-on.

Isadore dropped Jaxon off just before eight thirty so she could make it to homeroom. She smiled and gave Jaxon a hug that was stiff and awkward, as if Isadore wasn't used to giving hugs. Jaxon's reaction was the same. She wasn't used to receiving hugs.

"I know it's tough adapting to a new situation," her foster mother said. "But you're a strong girl to get this far, and I think you'll turn out just fine. You have heaps of potential." Isadore gave her another of her flat smiles.

Jaxon smiled in return. "See you this afternoon."

As she walked into the school, Jaxon thought about her foster mother. Isadore was a bit cold, and it was strange that she'd volunteer to take care of a kid in the system. She wasn't bad though, just a bit clueless. At least she was trying to help, unlike a lot of the "parents" she'd had to live with. But why did her idea of help have to include summer school?

Jaxon went to her locker and saw Courtney and some of her crew nearby. As luck would have it, Courtney's locker was only a few numbers down from her own. Jaxon always hit the jackpot like that.

As she got her books, Jaxon glanced at Courtney out of the corner of her eye. The girl was talking in a hushed voice with a guy and two other girls. The guy passed over some money, which disappeared into Courtney's purse. Courtney reached into her locker with exaggerated casualness and pulled her hand out, closed but seemingly holding nothing. Her and the boy's hands briefly met. A moment later, the boy put his hand in his pocket.

Jaxon's eyes widened. So Brett was telling the truth. Courtney really was selling drugs from her locker.

Courtney glanced over in Jaxon's direction, and Jaxon acted as if she was flipping through her math book. Suddenly someone bumped Jaxon from behind, and the book fell out of her hands.

"Courtney says mind your own business if you know what's good for you," some girl whispered into her ear.

Jaxon looked at the stranger, her heart pounding. The girl glared at Jaxon and stalked off.

*Great. I have enemies I haven't even met.*

At lunch, Jaxon sat alone as usual. The dining hall had typical long tables where everyone sat together. Jaxon figured it was to help with a sense of community and that "old school spirit." It also made it twice as obvious when you were being excluded. The nearest person to Jaxon sat three seats away.

She wished she could zone out to some music, but her foster parents had taken her phone. So she just kept her head down and ate her lunch, which turned out to be undercooked pasta and bland tomato sauce with a tasteless roll. It seemed school food was bad even in rich schools. Maybe there was some Universal Law of Grossness that applied to school food. She'd have to ask her science teacher about that.

"Hey, is this seat taken?"

Jaxon looked up. Brett stood across from her, holding his tray and grinning. He sat down before she could answer.

"Don't you have a golf game or something?" she asked.

Brett laughed. "No, that's after class. We don't have a golf course here at the school, although we should. We all drive over to a country club not far from here. Want to come and watch me play?"

"No, there's some paint I want to watch dry."

"That's not nice," Brett said with a smile.

"You're right. I shouldn't compare watching paint dry to watching golf. It's unfair to paint."

Brett laughed again. Jaxon was beginning to find his laughter annoying. Did he find everything funny, or did he just laugh as an automatic reaction?

"So why do you like golf so much?" Jaxon asked.

"I don't, really. Sure, it's a challenge, but it's not as fun as basketball or football. Mostly I do it for the business connections."

"Business connections?"

"Well, not yet, but my father says you have to play a good game of golf in order to fit in at the country club. When I inherit Dad's company, I'll need to be good on the golf course. That's where the real deals get made, not in the boardroom."

"Of course. How silly of me to ask." Jaxon sighed, stirring her unappetizing pasta with her fork.

"So which country club do your parents belong to?" Brett asked.

"None."

Brett looked appalled. "None? Are you sure?"

"No. I don't know. I mean, I don't care."

Brett looked confused. Jaxon suspected that, just like with Courtney, that happened often.

"People are saying that the woman who drives you to school isn't your mother, but it's not the kind of car a chauffeur drives. Besides, you sit in front. I saw you come in today."

Jaxon shook her head in wonder. Country clubs? Chauffeurs? Unbelievable.

"It's complicated," she said, trying to avoid the question.

"I like complicated women."

Jaxon rolled her eyes.

Brett continued as if he didn't notice. "So what are you doing this summer? I'm stuck in summer school. Grades, you know."

"Yeah, I'm stuck in summer school too."

Brett grinned again. "Hey! You know everyone is in the same classroom? We'll have the whole summer together."

"Wonderful. I can't wait."

Jaxon hoped her sarcasm would put him off, but it didn't. He seemed unstoppable.

"Oh, you're not going to like this. Courtney will be in summer school too. She's got even worse grades than me."

"Fantastic," Jaxon mumbled, finishing off her pasta with supreme effort.

"Do you have a boyfriend?"

Jaxon looked up in surprise then down again. "I did. We kinda broke up last week."

"That's too bad," Brett said, not sounding as though he meant it. "What happened?"

"He... moved away."

"Oh. So, um, what are you doing this weekend?"

Jaxon shrugged. What did she do most weekends? Hide in her room playing games and listening to music. Music and games were out, thanks to Isadore. She guessed her lessons would continue though. If she had to spend a whole summer with Courtney, she would need a lot of meditation.

"Dunno. Yoga and Aikido class. Not much else."

"Aikido, huh?" Brett made some karate chops in the air. "Training to be a ninja? Why don't I pick you up Saturday night, and you can show me some moves? Maybe I can show you some of my own."

Jaxon looked at him, appalled. "Where do you get these lines?"

Brett laughed with a trace of nervousness this time. "Lines? They're not lines."

Jaxon fixed her gaze on him. "They're lines, and they're lame."

Brett kept smiling. He really was unstoppable. "Come on. You're new here. Let's get to know one another. No strings attached. It's not a date or anything."

That last line told Jaxon it was totally a date. She was about to say no when something stopped her. Why should she say no? It wasn't as if she would ever see Otto again. Brett couldn't hold a candle to him, but at least he was friendly, which was more than she could say for the rest of the kids at this school. Sitting around in her room for yet another Saturday night didn't sound appealing. She'd had a lifetime of weekend nights alone. Maybe they could go out and see a movie or something. She hadn't seen a movie, or even TV, since she'd left the group home. Another of the Grants' stupid rules.

"Well, okay. But it's not a date," she said at last.

Brett put one hand on his chest and the other in the air. "Scout's honor."

"I seriously doubt you were ever a Boy Scout."

Brett laughed. "Of course not! My parents would never let me join. They said it's a waste of time when I could be learning how to play polo."

Jaxon rolled her eyes. Maybe another Saturday night alone wouldn't be such a bad idea.

"And there's a condition," she quickly added.

Brett cocked his head. Jaxon couldn't help but notice he had pretty eyes. A nice shade of blue. Not as crystal bright as hers—nobody had eyes like hers—but nice enough. The rest of him wasn't bad either.

"So what's the condition?" Brett asked.

Jaxon realized she had forgotten to speak. "No more cheesy pickup lines."

Brett laughed. "I keep telling you, they're not lines."

This time Jaxon laughed with him. "Whatever. Just stop with the cheesiness. And pick me up at eight. I have to ask my... parents' permission, but I'm sure I'll bring them around." Jaxon added a silent *I hope*.

"Cool. What's your number?"

"Oh... um... the battery was dead this morning, so my phone's at home. Just write down your number and I'll call you."

As Brett tore a page from his notebook and wrote it down, Jaxon sat back in her chair and smiled. Maybe this wouldn't be such a bad new life after all.

# Chapter 10

JUNE 6, 2016, MOJAVE DESERT, NEVADA

8:00 AM

"Don't believe half of what Edward tells you, honey."

Vivian and Otto were eating breakfast in the dining trailer. It had a small kitchen, a well-stocked pantry, and a rather cramped dining area. Vivian sat across from him at a table that was so small, their knees kept brushing against one another. She was wearing camo pants and a low-cut camo shirt that distracted Otto from his eggs Benedict.

Otto, to his embarrassment, was still wearing his prison jumpsuit. Yuhle had yet to go drive to the nearest town to buy him some clothes.

"It all seemed pretty convincing," Otto said.

Vivian nodded. "A lot of it is true, but Edward is so poorly socialized, he's not really in touch with reality. He grabs whatever he thinks sounds good and adds it to his belief system. Of course, that's how most people deal with the world, but Edward has a lot more material to work with."

"So how do you tell what's real and what isn't?"

Vivian grinned. "We're trying to figure that out. He's a genius though, and we need him. We'd be fighting blind without him."

Otto shook his head. "I don't get it. Yuhle is some big scientist, Edward is a computer maestro, you and Grunt are kickass mercenaries... where do I fit in?"

Vivian pointed at him with her fork. "You're the only person in the world who Jaxon trusts."

Otto felt something tug at his heart. He missed Jaxon terribly. In prison, he'd felt a cold emptiness, as if she had died. Now that he had the possibility of seeing her again, no matter how remote, he was filled with an anxious need to see her face and hear her voice.

Otto had never had trouble getting girls. He knew he was good-looking, and unlike a lot of kids who ended up in the system, he actually had social skills. Girlfriends came easily. There was something special about Jaxon though. He had sensed it immediately. When she had revealed her powers to him, at first he thought he'd been sensing them, that somehow he had guessed she was more than human. But he'd had lots of time in his cell to think about it, and he realized her unique abilities weren't what made her so interesting, before or even after he knew about them. Take away the super strength, the fast reactions, and that weird thing she could do with plants, and she was still special.

Sure, on the surface she was just another messed-up kid stuck in the system, another misfit with a bad attitude and no future. But under the surface was a hidden strength more impressive than the one she'd used to beat up half a dozen soldiers, or secret agents, or whatever they had been. Jaxon was depressed, withdrawn, and had trouble making friends, yet she somehow kept enduring. A life of being alone had made her rely on herself, and within the small little circle that made up her life, she was able to fight off all the rejection and hopelessness thrown at her and keep on going.

She was stronger on the inside than he was. He had good looks and an easy way with people, and he still screwed everything up. Grunt was right—he was a liability to the mission and to everyone around him. Most of all, he was a liability to himself. Jaxon had been through way more than he had, and she never lashed out. You'd never catch her setting fire to the neighbors' barn. As much as she'd suffered, she'd never taken it out on anyone.

"Penny for your thoughts," Vivian said.

"We have to save her," Otto replied, looking her in the eye.

"We will, honey."

"But how?"

"Edward has already located where she is. We got lucky. Normally the files for the Poseidon Project aren't accessible. General Meade—he's the man in charge—is paranoid. He won't even put the files on top-secret computer networks. He knows anything can be hacked if you have a good enough hacker. Edward thinks most of the files are in a single office on computers with no Internet access. If anything needs to be shared, an agent delivers an encoded memory stick that self-wipes if anyone tries to download information off it. So we only know as much about the Poseidon Project as Yuhle was able to learn while he worked there, plus a few other things we've pieced together."

"So how do we know where they sent Jaxon?" Otto asked.

"Your girlfriend is part of the California childcare system, so we have the address of her new foster family. Reading through those files set off a warning light in Edward's head. She was transferred way too fast, and her social worker was replaced. It looks suspicious. Yuhle thinks she's been sent to live with some of General Meade's agents."

Otto stood, bumping the table. "We have to get her out of there!"

"Easy there, hero. It's not that simple. First off, these are dangerous people, just as dangerous as Grunt and me. We could get hurt, or even worse, Jaxon could get caught in the crossfire. She's too important of an asset for them to let her go. If they saw they were going to lose her, they'd put a bullet in her brain without thinking twice."

Otto stood rooted to the spot. His entire body felt cold. "They'd do that?"

"Just as soon as spit."

Otto sat down. "So what do we do?"

"Bide our time. Scout out the situation. Get you trained up. We also have to be sure of our own security. Yuhle dropped out of sight after leaving the Poseidon Project, so we know that General Meade and his goons are looking for him to find out what he's up to. We seem to be safe here, but appearances can be deceiving. Grunt's checking on some things, Yuhle's checking on some things, and once we know for sure we're safe, then we can start thinking about saving Jaxon."

"I can't just sit here doing nothing!"

"You won't be doing nothing, honey. You're going to be learning how to fight back," Vivian said.

"Let's get started."

A few minutes later, Vivian and Otto stood in an open area behind the cluster of buildings. The chain-link fence with its spools of barbed wire on top enclosed far more space than was actually needed, and now Otto realized they used the back lot as a firing range. Shell casings lay scattered on the ground, glinting in the desert sun, and farther out, the ground was pockmarked with small, blackened craters.

"How are you at baseball?" Vivian asked.

"Pretty good. I never got to be on a team or anything. The system has moved me around too much."

"Our first lesson is showing you how to use those flash and smoke bombs you saw at the breakout."

Otto grinned. "Those were cool."

"They're also illegal and expensive, so we're going to start with a dud."

Vivian pulled a small metal sphere from her purse. Sticking out of the top was a metal bar that curved around the side like the bent handle of a fork. Otto noticed a small pin with a loop on the end fixed in place on the top of the bomb. It looked like a miniature version of the grenades he'd seen in war movies.

"Okay, listen up because all of this is important," Vivian said. "See this white dot painted on the bottom? That means it's a dud used for training purposes. There's no explosive inside. It's just a metal sphere. For the moment, you only get to touch the white ones. Live flash grenades have a yellow dot. Tear gas grenades have a black dot. Incendiary grenades have a red dot."

Otto felt his heart race. Would she train him with incendiary grenades? He kept his mouth shut though. He didn't want to seem too eager, especially with Edward and Grunt riding him about his love of flame. He realized Vivian was still talking and tried to focus.

"So you pull out the safety pin like this, releasing the lever. As long as you grip the grenade and the lever, the bomb is still safe. As soon as you throw it, the lever flies free, thanks to a spring inside. That primes the bomb. Then you have two seconds before it goes boom. Watch me."

Vivian hooked a finger through the ring of the safety pin and yanked it out. She threw the bomb, and the curved lever on the side flew free with a sharp "ping" as soon as she let go. The bomb arced through the air and landed about twenty yards away.

"Now with these flash grenades, you want to look away as soon as you throw. They'll temporarily blind you if you're closer than ten yards, but even up to a hundred yards, they'll dazzle you a bit. You don't want an afterimage floating in front of you and hampering your vision when you're in a combat situation. There's also a loud boom and some smoke and a concussion effect, like you noticed when we sprung you from jail. If you're within five yards, you'll get knocked off your feet. If you're within one or two yards, you'll get knocked unconscious, even if you're Grunt."

"Are they lethal?"

"Not generally. I suppose they could make someone fall off a cliff or give them a heart attack or something, but they're designed as nonlethal weapons. Riot police use them. They're designed so no fragments come flying off, unlike with regular grenades. Grunt and I aren't in the business of killing people. Well, not anymore."

Vivian retrieved the grenade and replaced the safety pin and lever. Then she laid out a circle of stones and walked back.

"Okay, that circle is your target. Try to throw it inside." Vivian handed him the dud bomb.

The target was about twenty-five yards away and a yard across. Pulling the pin out like Vivian had showed him, he threw the bomb. The lever released, and the bomb sailed through the air, landing just outside the circle.

"Not bad for a first try, but you forgot something," Vivian said.

"What's that?"

"You forgot to look away."

"It's a dud. I don't need to."

"If you're practicing something, practice it right. Otherwise you might not get it right in a combat situation. This isn't a game, Otto. Sooner or later we're going to be up against some pretty tough *hombres*."

Otto remembered the men who had attacked him and Jaxon in the greenhouse. If it hadn't been for Jaxon's abilities, they would have been prisoners in about five seconds.

And then what would have happened?

It seemed so strange that a sixteen-year-old girl could have strength and speed like that. The more he thought of it, the more he realized how little he knew about the real world. He was like a sheep being led around by people who knew the real truth, just like that nerd with his computers and conspiracy theories said.

"So if Atlantis is real, or at least Atlanteans, what else does Edward get right?" Otto asked.

Vivian made a face and shook her head. "Too much. I wish he was wrong more often."

"JFK?"

"Ha! You don't have to be a conspiracy theorist to know something was up with that. The president gets assassinated by a guy who, at the height of the Cold War, defected to the Soviet Union then was allowed back into the country, and then the assassin gets killed by a member of the mafia. You don't think that sounds fishy? And those are just the undisputed facts. There's a whole bunch more. Ask Grunt about the bullet trajectory. There's no way only one shooter was involved."

"Um, okay. What about the moon landing. Did we really go in 1969?" Otto asked.

"Yeah, we went. Edward is a bit loopy on that one. He's seen so many conspiracies turn out to be true he can't discriminate anymore. Doesn't help that he's locked up in that room all day, lapping that stuff up."

"So we didn't go to the moon in a UFO in 1957?"

"Or '58. He loves those little details. Makes him feel like he's being scientific. Don't worry, honey, the world is a lot weirder than you think, but it's not as weird as what's inside Edward's head. You should make friends with him. He could use someone like you."

"I'm not exactly well adjusted myself," Otto said with a wry smile.

"Maybe you should try harder."

Otto looked at his feet. "Yeah, I kind of messed everything up. Even though I didn't burn the greenhouse, I probably would have burned something else sooner or later."

"Rewrite the script."

"Huh?"

"Rewrite the script," Vivian repeated. "You got a movie in your head where you're a screw-up and can never make something out of yourself. You think that way and you'll be right, so rewrite the script."

"Yeah, like it's that easy."

"You have a lot to unlearn. Not surprising with an alcoholic mother and a dad who's always cheating on her."

Otto gaped. "How did you know that?"

"Edward hacked the files of all your therapists."

"And you all read them? Great."

"We had to know who we were dealing with. Trust me, you aren't nearly as messed up as Jaxon."

"So you all had a big laugh at my expense."

Vivian shook her head. "Ain't no one laughing, honey. Well, maybe Grunt did a little. He's like that. Edward sure didn't. He never mentions his parents or any of his family. Not once. In fact, I don't even know his last name."

"What about you?" Otto asked.

"What about me?" Vivian raised an eyebrow.

"What's your story?"

"Stick around long enough, and you might find out."

Otto sighed. "We make quite a crew."

"Sure do. Now practice throwing that a few more times before I trust you with live ordnance."

Otto did as he was told, getting the feel of the grenade. It wasn't like throwing a baseball. The bomb was smaller and heavier, and the lever made the grip a bit different. After about a dozen throws though, he was hitting inside the circle every time. He also remembered to look away.

"Now let's play with the real thing, honey." Vivian handed him another bomb from her purse. It had a yellow dot on the bottom, indicating it was a live flash grenade.

"Wow," Otto said, looking at the little bomb in his hand.

"No different than the dud, honey, except you better not drop it after you pull out the pin."

Otto grinned, pulled out the pin, and threw it at the circle. The instant before it landed, it burst in a blinding flash, a loud bang, and a puff of smoke. Otto took in a sharp breath of air. He had done that?

He blinked. A bright purple afterimage hung in front of his eyes, obscuring his view.

"You didn't look away, did you?" Vivian said.

"Ah... no. Sorry," Otto said, rubbing his eyes.

"I know it looks pretty, honey, but we're in serious danger. You have to do things right, or you'll end up dead. These guys don't play around."

The hum of the gate opening made Otto and Vivian turn. A Subaru pulled up the driveway. Yuhle got out, closed the gate, parked the car, and walked toward them.

He was carrying several shopping bags. "I got you some clothes, Otto. Time to get out of that prison jumpsuit."

"Can I burn it?" Otto grinned. The looks on Vivian's and Yuhle's faces told him he had used a poor choice of words. "Ah... I mean, can I throw it in the trash?"

Yuhle shook his head. "Keep it. You never know when something like that may turn out to be useful." The scientist set the shopping bags at Otto's feet. "I got you a bunch of clothes in the sizes you gave me. Hope you like them."

Otto pulled out a T-shirt that said "My family went to the Mojave Desert and all I got was this lousy T-shirt." He looked at Yuhle. "You hoped wrong."

Yuhle grinned and pulled out another T-shirt. It said "Property of Alcatraz. Shoot on sight."

Vivian giggled.

"Very funny," Otto said, rummaging through the rest of the clothes. There was a decent pair of jeans, a couple of loud Bermuda shorts that gave him a worse afterimage than the flash bomb, and a few more T-shirts that were about as stylish as the first two.

"Hey, it's better than what you got on now, honey," Vivian said.

"Good point," Otto grumbled and headed to his trailer to get changed.

# Chapter 11

JUNE 6, 2016, PENTAGON
BUILDING, WASHINGTON, DC

10:10 AM

"Thank you for flying all the way up here on your busy schedule, General Meade."

"My pleasure, sir."

General Meade stood at attention in front of a semicircular table, behind which sat the joint chiefs of staff. He had been called to Washington to discuss the Poseidon Project, and that made General Meade nervous. You were never called to the Pentagon unless there was trouble, and considering his project's slow pace, he knew what that trouble was.

Gunfire didn't bother him. His helicopter flying through a hail of RPG rounds was something he'd accepted as a part of life. Budgetary reviews, however, made him sweat under the collar.

One of the generals leaned forward. "We're here to discuss your project to isolate and utilize the Atlantis gene. How is it progressing? The super soldiers you promised us are still in the early development stage, are they not?"

General Meade continued to stand at attention. He hadn't been asked to sit. In fact, he didn't see a chair for him. The army liked all those little psychological jabs. He'd done them with the less competent among his own subordinates countless times. "Progress has been slowed by the unexpected loss of our lead scientist, sir. Dr. Yamazaki had quite a bad stroke and is in the hospital. We're continuing with our research."

Once again, Meade felt angry at himself for inducing a stroke in his star researcher. True, she had become rebellious and threatened the entire program, but Meade had acted hastily. While leaving her drooling in a hospital bed kept her from damaging his plans, it also slowed down progress. He should have tried other methods to bring her in line. Breaking a valuable tool wasn't wise. He needed to proceed more carefully.

"Quite expensive research, I see," one of the other generals murmured loud enough for General Meade to hear and obviously for his benefit. The officer was leafing through a file. "Forty-two million dollars and counting, plus another twenty-three million in requests in this fiscal quarter alone. And all this for just six subjects, all of whom are in suspended animation and not being trained."

"There is a seventh subject, sir."

"Ah yes," said the officer, not bothering to look up from his report. "A sixteen-year-old girl. We already approved the funding request and tied up a pair of useful agents for the next two years on that side project."

"She's very promising, sir. Young enough to be molded to our will. I know it's expensive, but—"

The officer closed the file folder with a snap and looked at General Meade for the first time. "The current administration has forced us to make significant budgetary cuts thanks to the most recent economic downturn. Our forces are already overstretched dealing with the Islamist threat in a dozen theatres of operations, plus we've had to bolster our support for our allies in Eastern Europe to deal with a renewed threat from Russia, and expensive research and development is taking place for the next generation of aircraft carrier. Funding your project has become increasingly difficult."

Another general opened a file folder. "Take this item here, for instance. Half a million dollars for a holding tank for the seventh subject, yet instead of using it, you've decided to spend even more money having her raised by a pair of our agents."

"It seemed the best course of duty considering the circumstances. At first we thought we'd capture her, but given her age, we decided to raise her and guide her into being a willing recruit," General Meade replied, thankful the general had been too polite to bring up the fact that half a dozen of his agents had been beaten up by a teenage girl. Then he remembered that one of those agents was the general's cousin. The general wasn't being charitable at all—he was just embarrassed.

"And how about this item here? Ten thousand miles in flight time on military transport planes for your personal use when conference calls would have done just as well."

"We need to have the utmost secrecy, sir. I suspect the Poseidon Project is being monitored by enemies of the state, including a defector with possible ties to treasonous activities."

And so it went for two grueling hours. At last they released him, telling him in no uncertain terms to bring back some results within a month or they'd pull the plug.

Stupidity bordering on treason! Did those idiots think they'd destroy the beings who piloted those UFOs by pacifying the Middle East and building a new aircraft carrier? The alien threat was beyond human and needed to be faced with a weapon that was beyond human. General Meade's team couldn't even begin to estimate how powerful an army of Atlanteans would be. It was the nation's only hope.

General Meade stormed out of the Pentagon, heading toward the nearest air force base. He was taking a plane to Los Angeles to meet with the team dealing with the Jaxon Andersen case. Yes, another flight logged when those bean-counting bureaucrats would rather have him make a conference call any advanced hacker could listen in on. Those fools had been stuck in Pentagon meetings and DC dinner parties for so long, they'd forgotten what war was.

They'd find out soon enough.

Within half an hour, General Meade was in the back of a C-5 Galaxy transport plane headed for Los Angeles. His mood had calmed, replaced with a steely determination. The top brass wanted results? Fine, he'd give them results.

But first he had to sort out this annoying kid and make sure she would be under his control when the time was right.

The plane landed in Los Angeles in late afternoon, and Meade spent the rest of the day working in an office lent to him by the air force base. It was too late in the day to have a meeting with his agents. His best assassin and best poison specialist were playing Mommy and Daddy to a kid who didn't know she was descended from the people of Atlantis. He'd find it funny if it wasn't so damned important.

The next morning, he met them at the air base.

General Meade, Stephen and Isadore Grant, Marquis D'Arcy, and Juliette Roan sat around a conference table. He wasn't going to make them stand like a bunch of privates just out of boot camp. Building a sense of teamwork was more important than asserting his authority. Respect had to be earned, not demanded. That was something else those Pentagon bureaucrats had forgotten. He opened the meeting by asking Jaxon's foster parents for a progress report.

Stephen spoke first. "She's a bit cold and aloof. I suspect that's normal after having been shuffled through the system all her life. She seems interested in my greenhouse though."

"Have you tested her skills? You reported that one of her special powers might be related to plants."

"Her psychologist mentioned she was working on a plant growth serum.

Judging from my chats with her, Jaxon doesn't have any more knowledge about science than your average high school student, so it's likely that's one of her special powers. I haven't brought her into the greenhouse though. I want her to feel more comfortable with me first. She's wary of me, I can tell. Most likely another legacy of her time in the system."

Isadore cut in. "She's cold with me too, especially after I took her phone. She's remained reasonably pliable, however. I think she'll make a good subject. I've seen her in class with Marquis, and she'll make an excellent killer one day."

"I've been having trouble containing her anger," Marquis said.

"That will take time," Isadore replied. "You nearly made me laugh with all that talk about the virtues of nonviolence."

Marquis grinned at her. "She needs to learn to contain her killing ability before she can use it. Don't worry, she'll be catching up with our tally before she even graduates from college."

General Meade allowed himself a smile. She and Marquis had been on several missions together and had a friendly rivalry over enemy body counts. Last time the general checked, both were in the triple digits with Isadore slightly ahead.

Juliette leaned forward. "I feel the soft touch works better. She seems to enjoy meditation, and I think she's beginning to bond with me. Relaxation and gentleness are the two things she's been yearning for her entire life."

General Meade nodded in appreciation. Juliette was his most disarming agent, with a hippie-like demeanor and a voice that could put a raging bull to sleep. She was one of the best in the infiltration business because nobody could ever suspect her of stabbing them in the back.

The general shifted uncomfortably in his seat. "It sounds like all is going according to plan. Unfortunately, the plan has changed. The Pentagon wants results. They're getting heat from the White House about expenses, and a lot of programs are being cut. What with the war in the Middle East and upgrading our capabilities, there isn't enough money to go around. Put some pressure on this kid. Stephen, get her in that greenhouse and find out what she can do. Marquis, get tougher on the training, and Juliette, get her out of her shell."

Isadore's brow furrowed. "And what about me?"

General Meade gave her a wry grin. "You have the toughest mission of all. This kid is dying to have a real parent. You need to learn to be a mother. Get her to love you, and she'll do whatever we say." He suspected he had just given her the most difficult assignment of her career.

"That will all take time," Isadore said, looking uncertain. "If the joint chiefs want results quickly, they're going to be disappointed."

"Your team needs to focus on getting that whiney brat of yours up to speed. In the meantime, I have something else that will satisfy the Pentagon. One of our test subjects is going to come out of hibernation and start the testing phase. If all goes well, he might get his first mission soon."

Stephen leaned forward in his seat. "That sounds good, sir. By the way, Dr. Hollis, the therapist Jaxon used to have, the one who runs the Forever Welcome Group Home, he's been making inquiries."

General Meade frowned. "Suspicious little fellow, isn't he? Don't worry, I'll take care of him. We have another problem too. Someone sprung Otto Heike from jail."

Stephen looked confused. "Otto Heike? Oh wait, there was a line about him in our briefing. He was Jaxon's boyfriend in the group home. He's not important. Why would someone break him out of jail? Do you think Dr. Hollis is behind it?"

General Meade shook his head. "It was a professional job. One of the former Poseidon Project scientists, Dr. Yuhle, has disappeared. He wouldn't have the capability to arrange a jailbreak, but he has the contacts to hire people who can. I think we might just have an Atlantean terrorist group on our hands."

Marquis and Isadore looked at each other and smiled.

"We've dealt with plenty of terrorists before," Marquis said.

General Meade nodded. "And you might be called on to do the same with this group. First we have to find out where they are and who they are and why they would want Otto. In the meantime, get Jaxon under control. I have plans for her."

# Chapter 12

JUNE 7, 2016, LOS ANGELES

7:20 AM

"Jaxon, you have a birthday coming up on the eighteenth. What would you like to do?"

Jaxon and Isadore sat at the breakfast table. It was Saturday, and her foster parents had let her sleep in. At least to their definition of sleeping in. They had woken her at seven.

She rubbed her sleepy eyes and took another sip of the smoothie Isadore had made her. "Um, I don't know."

"Would you like to have a party?" her foster mother prompted.

"I guess," Jaxon said with a shrug. It was too early to expect her to think.

Isadore sighed. "It would be really nice if you could respond in something other than monosyllables."

"Sorry."

Isadore frowned then visibly controlled her impatience. "Well, at least 'sorry' has two syllables. In any case, I think it would be fun for you to have a party. Who would you like to invite? You must have made some friends at school. How about that Courtney girl you mentioned?"

"I think she's busy next weekend," Jaxon lied.

"Oh, that's too bad. Anyone else?"

Jaxon shrugged, suddenly feeling lonely. She didn't know anyone enough to bring them here. Nobody cared anyway. Then Jaxon remembered Brett. He was supposed to pick her up tonight, and she hadn't even called him!

"Oh, um, we can organize the party later, but I was wondering if I could go out tonight?"

Isadore gave her an unreadable expression. Jaxon had become quite good at figuring out what foster parents were thinking. Stephen and Isadore were proving tough, however. They always had poker faces, or a fake face.

"With whom?" Isadore asked.

"A guy from my school named Brett," she said and hurried to add, "plus some other kids. Girls. He—I mean, they—want to go to a movie or something."

Isadore paused. There was that unreadable expression again. Then she smiled. Although Jaxon could tell the smile was fake, she couldn't tell what real expression it masked.

"That's great that you're making friends! Of course you can go out," Isadore said. "You'll need to keep in touch though, and be back by eleven."

"Okay." That had gone better than she'd hoped.

Isadore gave Jaxon one of her flat little smiles and leaned in a little closer. "So... who's Brett?"

"Just a guy from school. There's a bunch of us going. I need to call them though. I didn't have my phone with me, so I couldn't give them my number since I don't remember it." Jaxon tried to keep the annoyance out of her voice but didn't quite manage.

Her foster mother didn't seem to notice though, and she went off to fetch Jaxon's cell phone. Jaxon watched her go, wondering where Isadore kept it. She hadn't told her, and Jaxon knew better than to ask. Her foster parents were a bit off when it came to stuff like that. They were secretive about a lot of things. Neither of them talked about their jobs much, which was strange. Most of her foster parents had talked about work too much. While Jaxon didn't really want to hear about Isadore's insurance job over dinner, it was weird that her work day never came up.

Isadore came back with Jaxon's phone and, to Jaxon's surprise, told her to keep it for the rest of the day. Once they were done with breakfast, Jaxon hurried up to her room and turned on her phone.

It was pathetic how happy she was to have her phone back. Not that she had many people to call, but everyone had a phone, and not carrying one in her pocket gave people yet another reason to think of her as strange. The corners of Jaxon's mouth turned down when she saw she had no new messages. Go figure. Lying back on her bed, she played a couple of her favorite games and let her mind wander.

The sound of feet on the stairs made her hurriedly turn off the game.

"You doing okay in here?" Isadore asked, poking her head inside her room.

"Yeah, just about to call my friends."

Isadore gave her one of her flat smiles. "That's great." She walked down the hall.

Jaxon stuck out her tongue at her now-empty doorway and grumbled, "How about a little privacy for once?"

She fiddled with her phone for a little while longer, checking some of her favorite movie websites. Then she felt an urge to check her photos. She didn't have many, but there was one in particular she wanted to see. It was the last photo she had taken—a selfie with her and Otto in the weight room at the old group home.

Regret tugged at her heart. He'd been great. Jaxon looked at his smiling face, his head leaning so close to hers. She'd been smiling too—a real smile, unlike the one she forced herself to wear so often.

Damn, she'd finally gotten a boyfriend, and everything got messed up. She'd never see him again. He was in prison, and she was about to call some other guy for a date.

She felt guilty about that, but what could she do? Otto was gone. They'd never see each other again. She didn't know what prison he was in, and even if she did, there was no way Stephen and Isadore would let her visit. Jaxon sighed. Time to move on. She'd done it a thousand times before, and it looked as though she'd have to do it again.

Her thumb hovered over the delete key. It would be best to start with a clean slate. Keeping fond memories of the past would only hurt her.

She clicked delete. On her screen popped up the question, "Are you sure you want to delete this image? Yes. No."

Her thumb went for "Yes." After a moment, she hit "No."

She looked at the photo for another minute then closed out her phone without deleting it. She could call Brett later.

After she had done her homework for the weekend, she decided she'd better call the guy. Delaying would only make it harder. She pulled out the piece of paper with Brett's number and dialed it. Brett answered after only two rings, making Jaxon wonder if he was a bit too eager, and they made arrangements for him to pick her up at eight and drop her off at eleven. He had his own car of course, but at least he was polite enough not to ask why she didn't.

Jaxon reminded herself to get some driving lessons. It would be good to know how to drive. Sooner or later she'd get to drive off into the sunset like she'd been fantasizing about all these years.

Jaxon hurried downstairs and found Stephen and Isadore reading in the living room. Suddenly she felt embarrassed. Sad to say, she had never been on a date and didn't know what to tell her foster parents. She shifted her weight from one foot to the other and tried to look Isadore in the eye. "So... um... they're going to pick me up at seven."

"That's fine," Isadore said, sounding unconcerned. "Be back at eleven like I told you, and call in sometime before that to let us know you're okay."

"Great, thanks!" Jaxon said. Maybe those two weren't so bad after all.

Stephen spoke up. "Hey, I still haven't shown you my greenhouse. Want to check it out?"

Jaxon shrugged. At least he wasn't grilling her about tonight. Stephen put his book aside and led her out back.

Suddenly she was nervous. Isadore hadn't come with them. This was the first time Jaxon had been alone with her new foster father, and she remembered that time with Mr. Spencer. Jaxon tamped down her nerves. Stephen didn't seem like a pervert, though you never could tell. She didn't want to end up snapping his wrist too. Who knew where she'd end up then?

The greenhouse stood near the back of the Grants' well-tended back lawn, surrounded by flowerbeds and rose bushes. It was much bigger than the one at the Forever Welcome Group Home. Stephen opened the glass door and ushered her inside. She was surprised to find herself in a tiny room with another glass door on the opposite wall.

"I use an air lock to maintain constant temperature control," Stephen explained. "I perform a lot of experiments right here. It saves time if I don't have to commute to the university lab every day. Saves me the stress of dealing with LA traffic too."

Her foster father opened the second door, and she stepped into the greenhouse. Jaxon gasped. A wave of humid heat washed over her. All around were palm trees and ferns and strange flowering plants she couldn't even name. A thick, cloying smell assailed her nostrils, a mix of a dozen flowers all at once.

All the plants were kept in orderly rows, each one labeled with a name in Latin and another in English, plus the region where it could be found. She walked slowly down the aisle, feeling as if she was sucking in the life of this place. It felt so rich compared to the sterile sidewalks and shopping malls of Los Angeles. The air was obviously filtered and missing the sharp tang of pollution that had bothered her since she'd arrived. Why would anyone want to live in a city when they could be surrounded by all this? No wonder Stephen spent so much time here.

She felt her muscles relax, more so even than when Juliette led her in meditation. This warm, leafy place made her feel as if she was snuggled under a cozy blanket.

"Be careful not to touch anything," Stephen warned. "Many of these plants are poisonous, and they're all part of various experiments I'm conducting."

Jaxon nodded silently and spent several minutes wandering along the three aisles of plants, staring in wonder at all the different varieties. There were large, sickly sweet red flowers from the Amazon big enough that she could have put her fist inside the bulb. Snaking, spiky vines from central Africa climbed up terraces, their cruel hooks glistening with something she suspected was poison. She also saw a few things that were familiar, including Venus flytraps. One of her science classes had had some of those. They had a pair of sticky pads that gave off a scent that attracted insects. The pads were surrounded by little spikes that were sensitive to touch. When an insect set down on the pad, it got stuck and the two pads closed like a mouth. Like every other kid in class, she'd found those fascinating.

Other plants she didn't recognize by sight but by name, like hemlock and nightshade. Both were poisonous, she remembered. In fact, all of these plants looked a bit dangerous, or looked suspiciously safe, like that bush of tempting red berries.

"Um, you said a lot of these plants are poisonous, right?" she asked.

"Yes, they are," Stephen said from a few feet behind her. He had followed her through the greenhouse.

Jaxon tensed once again with the thought that they were alone in there. "Are they all poisonous?"

Stephen paused for a moment. "Well, yes. Some have contact poison, like this cactus over here, while others you have to ingest. Don't worry though. Most of them can't hurt a human just by touch. Plants generally go after insects, like those Venus flytraps, or have a toxin to ward off animals from eating them."

Jaxon turned to him, curious. "So why do you have so many poisonous plants?"

"I study them. It's one of my specialties."

"Why?"

Stephen smiled and looked away, studying a nearby cluster of yellow flowers. "Not all of these poisons have known cures, so that's one thing to figure out. Plus the chemical compounds themselves are interesting. You never know what you can turn them into if you concentrate them and learn to mass produce them artificially."

Jaxon's brow furrowed. The only thing she could think of that that would do would be to create more and bigger poisons, like for chemical warfare or something. But Stephen was the scientist, not her, so he could probably do all sorts of stuff with them.

"Come here," he said. "I have something to show you."

He led her to the far end of the greenhouse where there was a bed of soil with no plants in it. A shelf above it had a selection of seed packets. On the nearby wall hung various gardening tools.

"This is for you," Stephen said. "Dr. Hollis mentioned that you really enjoyed gardening. I've always found it relaxing myself, which is why I went into botany as a career. You can use this section of my greenhouse to do with as you like.

There are some basic instructions on the seed packets, and over here is an introductory book on gardening. You can set up your own garden and grow whatever you want."

"Wow, thanks!" Jaxon said, happy to have an excuse to hang out in here. It was much nicer than that uninviting mansion with its ugly art.

Then she became nervous. What about her weird ability? Back at the group home, she'd discovered that if she merely touched plants, she could make them grow faster than she ever thought possible. She'd actually seen plants grow a couple of inches as she held them. It was like magic. What was even stranger was she never used to be able to do that. While she'd always been a city girl, she'd touched grass and trees and flowers as much as anyone else. It wasn't until a couple of months ago that this unexplainable power had appeared in her fingertips.

Why? Why was she so different? She looked different, she was stronger and faster than an NFL linebacker, and now she had some sort of magic power over plants. What was she?

She realized her foster father was still talking.

"So I need to have a teleconference in my office with some researchers in Japan. I'll leave you alone to do what you want in here. Just remember to only work in this section and not to fiddle around with the other plants. Some can be dangerous, as I said. Have fun!"

"Okay, thanks again," Jaxon said with a smile.

As he walked away, she felt relieved and a bit guilty. She had been wrong to judge Stephen. Like his wife, he was a bit weird and distant, but deep down, he was all right.

Once she heard the greenhouse door close, she sat on a stool with the gardening book he had pointed out and skimmed through the first couple of chapters. As usual, her dyslexia slowed her down, the words getting jumbled in her mind. She shook her head in frustration. She could take on a bunch of grown men and kick their butts, but she had the reading level of a third grader. Why couldn't she just be normal?

She gritted her teeth and kept trying. Luckily the book had a lot of photos showing how things should be done, plus she had gained some experience at the group home. Once she felt as though she had gotten a handle on what she was doing, she went over to the seed shelf and looked over the bright photos of flowers and vegetables on the packets.

After a few minutes' thought, she decided to plant half the bed with flowers and the other half with vegetables. The bed of soil was six feet long and three wide, so she had enough room to grow plenty of both. The book said that vegetables took more room though, so she'd have to pick carefully.

She pulled a packet of carrots off the shelf. She puzzled through the planting instructions on the back, then she tore the packet open. Two dozen seeds were inside, each with a little green sprout poking out of them.

Jaxon blinked. They shouldn't be sprouting in the packet, should they? Had she done that? She shook them out onto her palm and watched, fascinated and repelled, as the sprouts lengthened before her eyes. "Damn it!"

She dropped them on the soil and stepped back. Looking at the heavy growth all around her, she shuddered. What would happen if she touched all this poisonous stuff? She'd better be careful.

Maybe this was a bad idea. Maybe she should thank her foster father and say she'd rather work on her homework or something.

But this greenhouse was so soothing—the warmth, the smells, even the soft sounds of the leaves and vines rustling in the breeze made by the air circulation system. It was wonderful. She knew she could be happy in here, just like in the greenhouse at the Forever Welcome Group Home.

She had to be careful though, or she'd be marked as different here too. Enthusiasm had gotten the better of her, and she'd picked up those seeds without thinking.

Hunting around, she found a pair of thick gardening gloves. She put them on and went back to her part of the garden.

"Looks like I have to run some experiments just like Stephen," she said with a chuckle.

She picked up one of the carrot seeds. As she watched, the sprout lengthened, but it grew much more slowly than when she held it with her bare hand. Putting it down again, she thought for a moment then went hunting around the greenhouse.

Five minutes' searching rewarded her with another pair of gardening gloves. She put on one pair over the other. It took her a few tries to pick up the seed again. Wearing two pairs of gloves was uncomfortable and awkward, but finally she managed to get a seed between her fingers.

She stared at it for a full minute. The sprout didn't seem to be growing. Nodding with satisfaction, she set to work.

It was slow going. The double gloves made her fumble and drop things, but even so, she made progress. Her mind relaxed and her worries slipped away as she dug holes for the seeds, placed them inside, and added a bit of fertilizer and water. Focusing on her work and her plans for the garden, she stopped thinking about all her troubles in life. Gardening took concentration, but at the same time, it was so simple. You encouraged things to thrive, to grow. Why couldn't the rest of the world be positive and nurturing like that?

The day slipped away as she planted, and it wasn't until several hours later that she heard the greenhouse door open. Jaxon hurriedly tossed the outer pair of gloves to one side so she wouldn't have to explain herself. Wearing only a single pair didn't make her look like a freak.

Stephen walked around the corner with a smile. "How's it going?"

"Great! I've divided the bed up into flowers and vegetables. I figured you guys would like some homegrown vegetables since you're health freaks—um, I mean health nuts. Sorry, I mean healthy." Jaxon blushed. Superpowers and no social skills. Why did she have to be such a mess?

Stephen didn't seem to notice. He bent over the soil, studying it carefully as if searching for something. "Looking good. Are you enjoying yourself?"

"Yeah! It's fun. I can see why you're so into this."

"Glad you like it. It's time to eat."

Jaxon's stomach grumbled. She had totally lost track of time. As Stephen led her out, she looked longingly at the greenhouse. She had to come back here often. These had been the most relaxing few hours she'd had in a long time.

That evening with Brett was a lot less relaxing.

Jaxon had no idea what to expect on her first date. Unlike every other sixteen-year-old in the country, she'd never been on one. That made her feel like a total loser, but at least nobody knew about it. One advantage of moving around so much was that no one knew her past. She could pretend her love life wasn't as lame as every other part of her life.

There was no pretending on this date though. While Jaxon didn't know what to expect, she hadn't expected it to be so boring. Brett was about as interesting as watching the Home Shopping Channel and ten times as fake. Nothing he said was the least bit interesting, and she couldn't remember a thing that came out of his mouth five minutes after he said it.

At least she was getting out of the house. That's what she kept telling herself as they buzzed around town. Brett tried to impress her by revving his Porsche and running red lights. When that didn't work, he bragged about all the golf games he'd won. That was an even bigger fail. They went to a burger place that was okay. Jaxon chowed down on a large burger with all the trimmings, plus a large order of fries and a large milkshake, to Brett's surprise. She thought with glee of what her foster parents' faces would look like if they could see her sucking in all that fat and salt and artificial flavors. Maybe they should try it sometime; it might do them some good.

After that, they went to a movie Jaxon wanted to see. Brett tried to put his arm around her the instant the lights went out, and she pushed it away. A few minutes later, the arm was back and she had to shuck it off again. Then an hour into the film, Brett went for broke. He plunked his arm around her and moved in. Jaxon turned toward him just in time to see a pair of puckered lips diving at her like some fighter plane about to launch a missile. She elbowed him in the ribs, pulling back on her abnormal strength. Mostly. With a surprised grunt, he moved away.

*Perhaps that's what I should have done the first time.*

He sulked through the rest of the movie and didn't share his popcorn.

At least Brett was good at his word and dropped her off just before eleven. After dodging a good-night kiss with a move that would have made her Aikido instructor proud, Jaxon waved good-bye with a massive sense of relief and went inside.

If that was what dating was all about, she'd give it a miss. It had seemed so fake, like, "Hey, let me feed you and show you a film so I can make out with you." Lame. What she and Otto had fallen into had been so natural. There had never been any artificial behavior or ulterior motives, just real attraction. They hadn't felt as if they had to go through all the motions before being boyfriend and girlfriend.

She sighed as she headed upstairs. Only the front hall light and the light in Stephen's office were on. Through the open door, she saw Stephen buried in his work, and he gave her an absentminded wave. Their bedroom door was closed and no light came through the bottom, which told her Isadore was already asleep. Jaxon smiled. That meant she got to keep her phone until morning. Stephen was too busy to ask for it and she wasn't about to give it up without being asked, so she hurried to her room and closed the door.

By the time her clock read 11:05, she was undressed and in bed, staring at the photo of her and Otto.

# Chapter 13

JUNE 8, 2016, ALBUQUERQUE, NEW
MEXICO

4:00 PM

General Meade was finally back where
he belonged—in the laboratory of the
Poseidon Project, getting his damn
scientists' butts in gear. Enough with
Washington bureaucrats, enough with
talking with his agents. The real action
was here, and he was going to make sure
that things progressed according to his
timetable for a change.

The general swiped his ID card, and
the laboratory door clicked open. After
making sure to close it behind him so
the automatic lock would keep the lab
secure, he passed a battery of computers

and equipment on his way toward a desk. At the desk sat a portly middle-aged man clicking away at a computer. The fellow glanced over his shoulder, spotted General Meade, and immediately deleted a screen. For a second the general thought he saw Facebook, but it was gone too quickly to tell, replaced by a gene coding sequence.

"So how's my star scientist?" General Meade asked, making his voice a little louder than necessary.

Dr. Patrick Jones was a prominent scientist and the new head of research at the Poseidon Project, but he wasn't at Dr. Yamazaki's level in either raw intelligence or work ethic. In fact, the guy was a bit of a blunderer. Easily intimidated though, and that was always a plus. Jones wouldn't dare try to backstab him like Dr. Yamazaki did.

"Things are going very well, sir," Dr. Jones said, giving an awkward salute. Jones was a civilian, but for some reason, he thought he was in the army now. "I've found out some interesting things. Analyzing the characteristics of the six subjects, I've found that each has increased strength and intellect. Their brain synapses are incredible. They have twice as many connections as the average human, and some of those connections are strange."

"Strange?"

Dr. Jones nodded, looking uncertain. "Most of the connections are along the normal neural pathways, enhancing them. It's like our synapses are a two-lane country road and theirs are an Interstate freeway." The scientist smiled as if proud of his metaphor, then he went on. "Some of the other pathways don't follow the regular routes. Since they've never been seen before, there's no good way to tell exactly what they do. Many of them go deep into areas of the brain we don't really understand."

"Could these be some sort of special powers?" General Meade asked.

"Not sure what you mean by special powers. They might have increased memory or something like that. It's impossible to tell without waking one up though."

"The missing subject, Jaxon Andersen, may have some sort of mental effect on plants."

Dr. Jones looked surprised. "Plants? That's odd. What sort of effect?"

"Witnesses say she can speed up their growth to a remarkable degree."

Dr. Jones thought for a moment. "That sounds more magical than biological. So far, everything we've seen from these subjects can be explained through biology. The increased strength and speed are simply enhanced neuromuscular development. Affecting plants goes way beyond that. Are you sure the witness is reliable?"

"It's something worth checking up on," General Meade said. "Perhaps it's some sort of transfer of energy from one body to another?"

"I don't know any mechanism that could account for that," Dr. Jones replied with a dismissive shake of his head.

General Meade felt an increasing annoyance. This scientist was deferential and scared when he was talking to General Meade about the project, but as soon as they got into scientific territory, he acted superior. That was a common and annoying trait among scientists and engineers—they thought they were smarter than they were and spoke arrogantly about their specialized knowledge. Well, General Meade knew a few things that would make this second-rate technician faint.

Controlling himself, General Meade went on. "I want you to investigate the possibility of all special powers. Throughout history there have been reports of abilities such as ESP, telekinesis, and out-of-body experiences. Perhaps these are linked to the Atlantis gene."

Dr. Jones barked out a laugh. "Next you'll be asking me to believe in UFOs!"

"Just do your job!" General Meade snapped.

Dr. Jones paled and sat bolt upright in his chair. "Y-yes, sir."

"Look, Jones, I've got to tell you I'm not impressed by your performance so far. The project is way behind schedule. I know you were brought in late and it takes time to get up to speed, but this is important. You've only brought in three new subjects since you've joined us. Where are the rest?"

Dr. Jones took a moment to collect himself. "That's something I wanted to talk to you about, sir. A lot of the likely matches for the Atlantis gene are missing."

"Missing?"

"As in missing persons. I was having trouble tracking down more prospects from the list you gave me. I've been cross-checking with documents like school and medical records to find matches based on physical appearance and known Atlantean traits, but many of these people's records simply stop. Then I ran a check with police records and found many are listed as missing persons."

General Meade's brow furrowed. He leaned over the computer screen. "Show me."

Dr. Jones clicked on a few keys and brought up a long list of names, each with a few paragraphs of information and a thumbnail image. General Meade's eyes scanned the images. Seeing all of them together really brought it home. Every one of them looked like all races at once. Sure, some may be simply mixed race like a lot of normal humans, but that blending of human attributes was obviously an Atlantean trait. General Meade wondered if, back in the distant past, the Atlanteans had been the ancestors of all races. They knew so little of the history, only hints and rumors, and they were only just beginning to learn about the biology. What secrets would they eventually uncover?

The scientist's voice broke him out of his reverie. "Here we go. Take this one, for example. Andrew Warner, Wisconsin high school football all-star and junior weightlifting champion. Adopted after being abandoned at birth. Interesting parallel to Jaxon Andersen, isn't it? Reportedly ran away from home three years ago and hasn't been seen since. Odd since he had a full football scholarship to Princeton for the next year. Who gives up a free ride to an Ivy League school? And here's another. Brianna Osborne, thirty-two, Canadian marathon runner, disappeared without a trace last year. No ransom note, no suicide note, no body. And the Fergusons, a family of five from Maine, all went missing six months ago and haven't been seen since. Their bank account was emptied the day before they went missing. And there are more— plenty more. A total of ninety-seven are missing, including that family of five and another family of three. The rest are lone individuals, either orphans or unmarried adults. None of them have been found."

General Meade rubbed his jaw. This was disturbing. He tapped through Jones's database. After reading a few more entries, something struck him. "All the missing person's reports are recent."

Dr. Jones looked surprised. "Really? Let's check." He entered a few commands to isolate the dates of when each subject disappeared and arranged them in chronological order. "So they are! The first went missing only four years ago. Most have gone missing in the last two years. It looks like the rate of their disappearances is increasing."

General Meade felt like slapping the idiot. Jones had assembled this database and hadn't seen a trend Meade spotted in a couple of minutes? This guy couldn't hold a candle to Yamazaki. What a waste to scramble her brain like that.

Idiots everywhere! How the hell was he going to save the world when he was surrounded by idiots? The general fought to control himself. Getting angry would only be counterproductive. Somebody or something was taking the Atlanteans. He needed to find out why.

"Put each disappearance onto a map," he ordered.

Dr. Jones did as he was told. After a few minutes, the map showed disappearances in every region of the United States and Canada, with a dot for each missing person. So far the Poseidon Project had limited its search to those two countries for convenience's sake, but Meade had the dreadful feeling that it might be happening globally. He studied the map for a moment, looking for trends.

Jones said what Meade was thinking. "It looks like they're going missing everywhere. Slightly more disappearances in the Northeast and California and fewer in the Midwest, but that could be explained by differences in the general population. We've already noted that the Atlanteans don't seem to cluster geographically. They're spread out evenly in the regular human population."

"So whoever's doing this is spread out too, or traveling constantly."

Jones color-coded the dots by year and still found no obvious trend. "It looks like you're right, sir. Now what do we do?"

*Damn good question.* Someone was obviously taking the Atlanteans and had been doing so since the early days of the Poseidon Project. Could it be an inside job? He doubted it. For the first three years, the research had been very basic and all done by Pentagon scientists. Their loyalty wasn't suspect, and in any case, they were all under close observation. When he had gotten the funding to kick the project into high gear, he brought in Dr. Yamazaki. While she might have leaked some information before her "stroke," that was well after the start of the disappearances.

Could the research itself have alerted some outside agency? Pentagon operatives had gone out and asked plenty of questions, even monitored some suspected Atlanteans. That might have been noticed. General Meade knew America was filled with spies. The Russians and Chinese had small armies of operatives working in various capacities. Even allied countries such as Israel and France kept a close eye on the world's largest superpower. That was how the game was played, and General Meade didn't take it personally. Could some other nation, hostile or friendly, be trying to get their hands on the Atlantis gene? Or perhaps one of the major pharmaceutical or biotech companies? With the economic downturn, corporate espionage was at an all-time high. While he wanted the Atlantis gene for its military applications, he couldn't even begin to imagine its economic potential.

He'd have to investigate these disappearances. Unfortunately, that meant getting more funding from the Pentagon, and that wasn't going to happen.

If some organization had been collecting Atlanteans for years longer than he had, and had gathered them in much greater numbers, that organization's research was probably far ahead of the Poseidon Project.

When an enemy is potentially stronger, the best thing to do is to strike first.

"Dr. Jones, when can you wake the first subject out of hibernation?"

The scientist blinked. They hadn't even discussed doing that yet. "But, sir, we haven't finished with our tests!"

"I'm aware of that. How soon can you wake one?"

"Um, today if you wish, but—"

"Do it."

Dr. Jones shrugged, obviously flustered.

"Which subject do you think is the best suited to wake up?" General Meade asked.

"Um… probably Zion Wilson," Dr. Jones said, clicking on his computer again and bringing up several files. "He's been the most responsive to the chemicals we've been pumping into him. Plus he's the youngest of the subjects, not that that seems to make much difference with these Atlanteans. Even our oldest, who's in her mid-fifties, has more strength than your average Marine."

"Impressive, but we want the best of the best."

Dr. Jones turned to him curiously. "What for?"

General Meade glared at him. "Shut up and get to work."

The scientist cringed, and the general allowed himself a moment of smug satisfaction. Jones was weak, and Meade despised weakness. It was everywhere—in the Pentagon, in the White House, and it was rampant in civilians. America used to be strong. Now everyone just wanted to go shopping, play games, and stuff their faces with fast food. It had become a nation of overgrown children. That needed to change, and it looked as though he had to be the man to change it.

Meade followed the scientist past some complex equipment whose function Meade only vaguely understood. There, along the far wall, stood seven metal pods, each eight feet tall. The one on the end was empty and stood open. Its interior was padded, and various nozzles and sensors filled in spaces between the padding. The other six were closed and occupied. Computer monitors next to each of them showed the occupant's vital signs, such as their heartbeat and blood oxygen levels. Through small windows in each pod, they could see the sleeping faces of half a dozen Atlanteans.

General Meade paced slowly down the row. Three men and three women, all in suspended animation, their eyes closed, minds unconscious. Like with the computer database, seeing their physical similarities when they were all bunched together was striking. All had dark skin that the casual observer would label as black, but their genetic makeup was more complex than that. Their facial structure was wide with high cheekbones, like the Native Americans, and their eyes had traces of epicanthic folds like the Asians. If the eyes were open, Meade knew they would all be a brilliant blue that spoke of northern Europe.

As Dr. Jones went to one of the tanks and studied the monitor, Meade wondered what these people's ancestors had been doing for the past few centuries. They'd been hiding in plain sight, their powers unnoticed. How could that have happened?

Suddenly the answer hit him—their skin color! For most of America's history, the Atlanteans would have been dismissed as second-class citizens, or worse, slaves. No one would have paid much attention to them except to order them around. Being the victims of prejudice, they would have quickly learned to hide their powers and stay nondescript.

But perhaps not in all cases. At West Point, his professors had taught them about military history so the warriors of the future could learn from the great warriors of the past. One of the periods that had impressed him the most was the Seminole Wars in nineteenth-century Florida. According to the history books, the Seminole rebels were a mix of escaped slaves who married into the Seminole tribe. They were described as a blend of white, black, and Native American. Hiding in the depths of the Florida swamps, they fought off every army the United States sent at them for the better part of a century. Entire regiments had disappeared without a trace.

What if the Seminoles had been Atlanteans? Hidden as they were in the almost impassable swamps, they could have used their powers without fear of discovery. It would also explain why they hadn't died from the alligators, poisonous snakes, and diseases that plagued the region. And when regiments of US soldiers waded in to defeat the tribe, the Atlanteans would have leapt out in ambush, their unnatural strength and speed tearing through the soldiers' ranks.

Meade tried to imagine what that had been like, seeing superhumans bursting out of the thick underbrush and smashing through lines of surprised soldiers. As more men fell, the soldiers would have panicked, their officers barking orders to try to keep them in formation before they too got cut down. It would have all been over in a few minutes. The Atlanteans would have been ruthless because they would have needed to kill them all so that none could get back to tell the tale. In so many of those battles, none did. Even if a few did make it back, their wide-eyed stories of Seminole warriors leaping ten feet in the air or cutting a man's body in half would have been dismissed as panicked imagination.

But what of other battles in other times? Had that been the only time the Atlanteans had banded together? What about Hannibal, the ancient North African general who had marched across Western Europe, defeating Roman legions along the way, to cross the Alps with an army of soldiers riding elephants to threaten Rome itself? The Carthaginians, as they had been called, had almost defeated the greatest empire the world had ever seen, yet history knew so little about them. The Roman revenge had been terrible. After decades of warfare, Rome got the upper hand and leveled the capital at Carthage, leaving not one stone atop another, and defaced every Carthaginian inscription they came across.

The defeat of the Seminoles had been just as brutal. The tribe had been slaughtered by an overwhelming force of troops, the adults killed and the children sold into slavery.

If only American generals had known how valuable the Atlanteans could have been, perhaps they could have struck a deal. There were so many enemies back then—other hostile tribes, the Mexicans, the British. And in the next century, there had been the Germans and Japanese and Koreans and Vietnamese and Iraqis. America had fought long and hard to become the world's biggest superpower and had lost countless brave men and women to do it. With the Atlanteans' help, perhaps the sacrifice wouldn't have been so great. Perhaps the path to world dominance would have been easier. Instead, the Atlanteans had been defeated without being recognized and appreciated for what they were.

How many times had that happened? History wasn't Meade's specialty since the concerns of the present were far more important to him. The past held the key to Atlantis though. He needed to learn more.

Dr. Jones's whiney voice broke him out of his thoughts. "Zion Wilson is ready to be taken out of hibernation, sir."

The scientist stood next to one of the suspended animation tanks. General Meade walked over and looked through the little window. The face he saw inside was a young man's, his features placid.

"Congratulations, Mr. Wilson," General Meade said. "You're going to be the next in a long line of warriors. But this time, you won't be fighting an empire. You'll be fighting to preserve one."

# Chapter 14

JUNE 8, 2016, LOS ANGELES

7:00 AM

The next morning, Isadore woke Jaxon at the usual horribly early hour.

"Hope you had a good time last night. Thank you for coming home on time. That shows responsibility, and that's essential for developing a healthy adult attitude."

"Ermph," Jaxon mumbled, her face buried in her pillow. She'd only caught a few words of what her foster mother had said. Something about healthy. She hoped that meant a smoothie. She probably had to do a bunch of yoga stretches to get it though.

"Get on up," Isadore went on in a fake cheerful voice that sounded like she'd stolen it from some old lady on a cooking show. "Let's start the day right with some yoga stretches."

Jaxon groaned, flipping over.

"I'll see you downstairs, sleepyhead!"

"Sleepyhead?" Jaxon mumbled into her pillow. "She's finally gone nuts."

Sleep threatened to pull Jaxon back into unconsciousness, and she had to force herself to stumble over to her dresser to get her yoga clothes.

Ten minutes later, they were in the exercise room as the morning light streamed through the window. Isadore led her in something called a sun salutation, which mainly involved a lot of squishing herself flat on the yoga mat then standing and stretching with her arms over her head. Her foster mother explained that it helped the circulation early in the morning and gave you energy for the rest of the day. For the Hindus in India, who invented yoga, it was also a way of showing respect to the sun as the giver of life.

Jaxon decided she would have a lot more respect for the sun if it rose about three hours later.

"You're sluggish today, Jaxon," Isadore observed. "What did you eat last night?"

"Salad," Jaxon lied.

"Is pizza the new salad? If you had eaten properly, you wouldn't be groaning every time you did a forward fold."

"I didn't eat pizza," Jaxon grumbled.

Her foster mother was right though. She could feel every bite of that burger. It was strange how she hadn't really noticed just how different she felt on her new healthy diet until she went back to her old eating habits. Maybe Stephen and Isadore were onto something. Later at breakfast, Jaxon felt grateful for the bowl of muesli and her usual smoothie.

As she scarfed them down, her foster mother said, "I went to bed early and didn't see you come back. Stephen said you came back on time though."

"Of course," Jaxon said, trying to look dutiful.

Isadore held out her hand. "I'll need your phone back. It's best not to get too distracted by the Internet and games."

Jaxon tensed. It was none of Isadore's business what she did with her phone. "Um, I wanted to make a couple of calls about the birthday party next week. Can I keep it until lunchtime? It's not like I can call my friends right now. They're probably still asleep."

Jaxon hoped Isadore would take the hint about the early mornings she was forcing on Jaxon. To her disappointment, Isadore didn't get it.

"Well, okay, I suppose you can keep it until noon. I'll just go turn the Wi-Fi off so you won't be tempted by all the nonsense online."

Isadore rose and left the room. Jaxon resisted the urge to flip her off.

"Yeah, wouldn't want to be tempted by something fun," she muttered.

Even though the Internet was off, Jaxon managed to sneak in a few games from among the ones saved on her phone. She wondered if Isadore knew about them or even realized that you could play games on your phone without the Internet. She and Stephen were really strange. Like, they were really knowledgeable about some stuff and completely clueless about others. What kind of lives did they lead where they could be so rich yet so disconnected?

Late in the morning, Jaxon decided to make a few calls. She knew she needed to contact Brett. People always called each other the day after a date, but she didn't know what to say. Should she call? She decided to text. That way she wouldn't be drawn into a conversation. But what should she say? Was she supposed to text first, or was he supposed to do it? She wasn't even sure she wanted him to text at all.

She decided to be the one to make contact. The next decision was what to say. "Thanks for a good time"? That might be too encouraging. "You're shallow and boring"? No, people didn't like honesty. Hmmm.

Aha! "See you on Monday.". No, a bit cold.

Or maybe, "See you on Monday. "

Maybe, "See you on Monday. ;-)"? No, a wink was too suggestive. A smiley face was friendly but not intimate. She didn't exactly dislike Brett—she just didn't like him. Jaxon found him boring while at the same time enjoyed the attention.

Did wanting attention from a guy you didn't like count as leading him on? Why did this stuff have to be so complicated?

She settled for, "See you on Monday. " Friendly but neutral. If Brett wanted to read something into it, that was his fault. She gritted her teeth when spellcheck showed her she had misspelled "you" and "Monday." Dyslexia was so annoying! She used autocorrect and reread it a couple of times to make sure autocorrect hadn't made her say something embarrassing. She didn't want this conversation to end up as a meme.

Less than a minute after she pressed Send, Brett texted her back.

"What are you doing today?"

Uh oh. Had the smiley face been too smiley? Maybe she shouldn't have put that in. She got busy texting, using auto-correct again to keep from looking dumb. It was bad enough having the smart kids in class think she was stupid, but Brett? That would be mortifying.

"Busy with my parents today."

As she hit Send, she felt a tug of sadness. Parents. What a pathetic lie. She'd never had any parents, just adults who took care of her for their own reasons. She still hadn't figured out what the Grants wanted with a foster kid, but whatever their motivations, it didn't make them her parents. All her life, she'd yearned to have a real mother and father, yet she didn't really know what that would be like. From listening to other kids talk, real parents were almost as annoying as foster parents. Jaxon couldn't believe it was that bad. Parents loved you, right? They'd always be there for you.

Except hers hadn't.

Jaxon felt an old familiar sadness in the depths of her chest. If parents loved you, why had hers ditched her at the front door of some clinic? Had they realized she was a freak even as a baby? No, that couldn't be it. She didn't even know about her own powers until she was nine, and hadn't discovered that thing with the plants until last month. So why had they abandoned her?

She had had endless conversations with her therapists about this. They always said lame things like maybe her mother was poor or on drugs and couldn't take care of her. Yeah, that sure made her feel better. Lots of poor parents keep their kids. And if her parents had been drug addicts, they should have loved her enough to quit instead of getting rid of her like last week's garbage. Even if they couldn't have gotten off the drugs, couldn't they have straightened themselves out later and come looking for her?

The other thing her therapists always said was that she had to accept the situation and use it to make herself grow stronger. Whatever that meant. How was being different and alone supposed to make her stronger?

Her phone blipped, telling her she had another text message. Brett again.

"Too bad ur busy, babe. See you on Monday. Miss you."

Jaxon rolled her eyes. Her parents didn't even know whether she was alive or dead, and the only person showing any interest in her was a rich idiot like Brett.

She tossed the phone back on her mattress then looked at it for a moment.

The reason she was getting to keep it was supposedly to invite people to her "birthday" party next weekend. Another lie. Who the hell was she supposed to invite? Brett? Too embarrassing. There was no one else at school to ask though.

Then she had an idea. Why not ask Ginger Edwards? She was stuck at the Forever Welcome Group Home, but if she could get her caseworker to arrange for the Grants to take Jaxon, who knew what else she could do? Maybe she could come down for the weekend. The group home gave out weekend passes to some of the kids if they were properly chaperoned and doing well with their therapy. It was worth a shot, and it would be nice to talk to her in any case.

She almost dialed Ginger's number before remembering that residents were only allowed to use their cell phones in the evenings. Jaxon wanted to call her now though. She wanted to talk to someone sympathetic, not just some guy who wanted to get into her pants or some foster parents trying to mold her into their image of a perfect teen.

Jaxon still had the number to the group home. Maybe if she called, they'd let her talk to Ginger. She hit the number, and Joyce, one of the nurses, answered.

"Hi, Joyce, this is Jaxon. Remember me?"

"Hello, Jaxon! Of course I remember you. How are you settling into your new home?"

"It's okay, I guess. Would it be all right if I spoke with Ginger?"

"Oh, Ginger got released the day after you did. Her parents came and picked her up."

"Oh, wow. That's cool. I can call her on her own phone then. Say hi to Dr. Hollis for me."

There was a moment's silence, then the nurse said, "I'm afraid Dr. Hollis doesn't work here anymore."

"What? Why not?"

"We're not sure why. He was asked to leave the same day you left," Joyce said, sounding nervous and guarded. "It was a decision by the state, and we weren't given a reason. I'm afraid I have to go now, Jaxon. Take care." The nurse hung up.

Jaxon stared at her phone in disbelief. What was going on? Dr. Hollis had been at that place for years. He'd even gotten an award for running it. It was on the wall right next to his desk. Why would they fire him?

She got a sinking feeling in the pit of her stomach. She knew why. They blamed him for the fire at the greenhouse.

Jaxon slumped back on her bed. This was so messed up! No one had believed her about the guys attacking her and burning down the greenhouse. Otto had been sent to jail for it, and now Dr. Hollis was being punished too. While he had been as clueless as the rest of her therapists, he was a nice guy and didn't deserve this.

Not that she could do anything about it. If Dr. Hollis hadn't believed her, there was no way some bureaucrat in Child Protective Services would.

She lay on her bed for a long time, feeling miserable and alone. At last she sighed and sat up. It was almost time for her Aikido lesson, and if she wanted to call Ginger, it was now or never.

Jaxon dialed her number, and after a couple of rings, Ginger's familiar voice came on. "Hey, kid, how are you doing down in Los Angeles?"

Jaxon grinned and rolled her eyes. Why did Ginger always call her "kid" when she was only sixteen? "It's okay, I guess. Heard you got out."

"Yeah, my... parents decided I was doing well enough to move back in with them."

"That was quick! They only just put you in there."

"I guess I'm good at convincing people to do what I want."

"Well, you sure did a good job with your caseworker. She got me into a mansion. Stephen and Isadore, those are my foster parents now, they're, like, millionaires."

"Cool! Glad you've landed a good place."

"Good but not great. They're total control freaks. I'm lucky to be able to call you. Hey, I don't have much time to talk, but I was wondering if you'd like to come to a party next Saturday? It's my birthday. I totally understand if you can't because it's down here in Los Angeles..." How pathetic was her life that she was asking a former roommate from another city to come to her birthday party?

"Yeah, I can come!" Ginger said. "I'm going to be visiting an aunt in Los Angeles next weekend, so you're in luck. It'll be great to see you again. I missed you."

Jaxon grinned from ear to ear and felt her heart swell. How often did someone say something like that to her? Never? "Awesome! I'll text you our address. It's going to be a small party though, like only us and my weirdo foster parents probably. I don't know anyone here yet, and the kids at school are all rich snobs."

"Never mind, Jaxon, we'll have a great time."

Jaxon smiled again then grew serious. "Hey, what's the story with Dr. Hollis?"

"What do you mean?"

"He got fired, right?"

"Oh, I didn't know that."

"You must have! Joyce said he got fired the same day you left," Jaxon said.

"Oh, right, um, sorry, I forgot. I don't know. They didn't say."

Jaxon's brow furrowed. Ginger sounded flustered, as if she had been caught in a lie. After a moment, Jaxon shook off that feeling. Why did she always have to be suspicious of people? Ginger was her friend.

"Never mind," Jaxon said. "Anyway, it'll be great to see you. I'll text you the address."

Isadore's voice interrupted her. "Jaxon, Marquis is here!"

Jaxon sighed. "Okay, Ginger, gotta go. Drop me a line later this week."

"Sure, see you Saturday."

Ginger hung up, and Jaxon put on her Aikido uniform. She really didn't feel like sparring with Marquis right now, but she saw no way to get out of it. She'd heard so much weird stuff in the last half hour that she needed time to wrap her head around it. Instead she'd have to deal with the frustration of trying to hit her martial arts instructor as he danced around her like a butterfly.

And that was exactly what happened. Like their first lesson, Marquis showed her some moves and asked her to try them on him. Most of the time she screwed up, barely even managing to touch him. The only time she could do it right was when he slowed down and let her win.

Jaxon felt her anger and frustration rise. All this crap she had to deal with in her life, and now she had to fight the Untouchable Man while her foster mother watched from the doorway with an amused smile. Why couldn't people just leave her alone?

She found herself thrown to the mat again. That always happened when she let her thoughts wander for an instant with this guy.

"You're not paying attention to your lesson," Marquis chided her. "That can be fatal in a real fight."

"Like I'm going to get in a real fight," Jaxon grumbled as she got up. "It's not like some psycho killer is going to attack me in math class."

"The world is a dangerous place. Get up and face me," her instructor ordered.

Jaxon sighed. "I'm sick of this. I can't beat you."

"You will if you pay attention and keep trying. Now try to hit me and avoid my counterattack."

Jaxon shook her head. What Marquis really meant was "keep missing me by a mile until I humiliate you by throwing you on the mat again." What was the point?

"Come on. You're just standing there," Marquis said.

Jaxon grumbled and threw a punch. Marquis dodged it easily. Why were they wasting her time with this? She threw another punch and missed again. It was so totally pointless. Another punch, another miss. No family, a pathetic fake birthday coming up—what was the point of any of it?

Jaxon missed again as Marquis danced around her. *Aaargh, this is so frustrating!*

Marquis grabbed her wrist and was about to throw her when she swore and lashed out. Her fist flew with lightning speed and landed square on Marquis's chest. He grunted and flew backward, tumbling over himself and rolling right off the mat. From her spot in the doorway, Isadore let out a cruel laugh.

Jaxon brought her hands to her mouth. "Oh my God, I'm sorry! Did I hurt you?"

Marquis lay curled up on the floor, clutching his chest. Suddenly his head whipped up and he snarled at her, hatred sparking in his eyes. Jaxon went cold and stepped back.

An instant later the look was gone, replaced with a serene smile. Marquis clambered awkwardly to his feet and nodded. "Good job, Jaxon, you're learning."

"I'm so sorry," Jaxon hurried to say. "Are you sure you're okay?"

"Yeah, I slipped. Let's continue with the lesson, shall we?"

Jaxon and Marquis went through several more moves, practicing flips and blocks, but it all seemed a blur. The only things she could think of were Isadore's barking, predatory laugh and Marquis's hateful, murderous glare.

# Chapter 15

JUNE 9, 2016, ALBUQUERQUE, NEW MEXICO

9:45 AM

"Is he ready?" General Meade asked, leaning over the examination table where Zion Wilson lay unconscious.

"Almost. I'm giving him a range of drugs to bring him out of his medically induced coma. I'm also giving him that special drug you shared with me from the Pentagon. It's amazing such a thing exists!" Dr. Jones said, filling a hypodermic needle and sticking it into Wilson's arm.

General Meade shrugged. The drug Jones was referring to was a memory suppressor. It had been developed during the Cold War to create sleeper agents in enemy nations. One injection would suppress all memory for up to three months. Special psychologists would then instill new memories into the subject, turning an American accountant into a Russian munitions factory worker or a US Marine into a Chinese soldier. That made them the perfect long-term spies because they themselves believed their roles. Even under torture, they couldn't reveal their true identities because they were convinced their cover story was true.

Giving them a new injection every three months was vital, however, or the old memories would start coming back and their artificial identity would fall apart. Part of their new identity was that they were diabetic. The "insulin" the Pentagon provided was actually harmless saline solution, except for one dose every three months that would be the memory suppressor.

Civilian scientists had been experimenting with memory drugs for years, and the savvier among them figured the military already had something far more powerful, as it did in optics, electronics, and chemical engineering. Dr. Jones, however, was not what anyone would call savvy. He was basically an intelligent idiot who worked well enough when set on a particular task and lacked the imagination or perspective to see beyond it. He would have made a good assistant to Dr. Yamazaki. Pity she had to be put down.

"When will he awaken?" General Meade asked.

"In a couple of hours. Then the reeducation can start."

Meade nodded and laid a hand on Wilson's bare shoulder. Strange that it felt no more muscular than a normal man's, yet this fellow could literally tear him in half. The perfect spy, the perfect soldier.

"You're going to be our archetype," General Meade said to the unconscious figure. "You're going to be the first of a new regiment in the finest army the world has ever seen."

"Once we get him trained up, he'll be the best soldier you ever had," Dr. Jones reassured him. "But who are you going to use him against? The Islamists? The Chinese?"

General Meade gave him a look that even Jones could figure out. The scientist wilted and got back to work.

Leaving the scientist to do his job, Meade went over to a spare desk on the far end of the lab. He pulled a laptop out of his briefcase and put in a thumb drive that an agent had delivered that morning. It was from Stephen and Isadore Grant—most likely a progress report. Meade had given them strict instructions only to communicate face-to-face or by couriered messages delivered by trusted agents. Now that someone appeared to be stealing Atlanteans, or perhaps even the Atlanteans were banding together, security was more important than ever.

The thumb drive contained a single .mov file. General Meade plugged in a pair of earphones, put the volume low to be on the safe side, and clicked it open.

Stephen Grant's rugged middle-aged face appeared on the screen. "Hello, sir. There have been some new developments in Jaxon's progress. Following your suggestion, I allowed her into the greenhouse. I'd set up a section for her to work on her own garden and hid a miniature camera just above it—one of those new models that looks like a nail sticking out of the wood. Anyway, she took the bait. Right from the start I could see she was entranced by all the plant life. She seems to have a real affinity for them, just like Dr. Hollis said. I decided to test her ability with plants by leaving her alone and encouraging her to cultivate something. What I found was amazing. It's best to see for yourself."

Stephen's face disappeared, replaced by a shot from his hidden camera. General Meade leaned in to get a closer look.

The shot was from above and showed the girl standing over an empty bed of soil. She handled a packet of seeds. After a moment, she opened the packet and poured the seeds into her hand. Each of them was partially sprouted, which was unusual.

General Meade's jaw dropped as he saw the sprouts grow within a matter of seconds.

Jaxon appeared shocked too and tossed them onto the soil.

Stephen's face came back. "Did you see that? The seeds grew right in her hand. After she went to bed, I dug them up and put them under the microscope. They look like they'd been sitting for a few days in good soil with plenty of water, but all she did was hold them. And the process began even before she opened the packet! I have no scientific explanation for this. Obviously the power is coming from her, as you suggested, but I have no idea how. We'd have to dissect her to solve this riddle, and maybe even then we wouldn't find out."

General Meade shook his head. Dissect her and lose a future soldier? No, you only sacrificed soldiers when it was absolutely necessary.

"Now look what happens next," Stephen said.

The film went back to the hidden camera. Jaxon walked away, and there was a jump, the time stamp in the upper right-hand corner showing that Stephen had cut a couple minutes of video. Jaxon came back wearing gloves. She picked up one of the seeds. General Meade leaned in closer to the screen, squinting to see the detail. It was hard to make out, but it looked as if the sprout was growing again, although more slowly this time. Jaxon's next action seemed to confirm this. She dropped the seed and walked away again. Another couple of minutes were cut, and she came back with a second set of gloves. She put them on over the first pair, picked up the seed a second time, and stared at it for a while. It didn't appear to grow. Looking satisfied, Jaxon got to work on her garden.

The film cut back to Stephen's face. "After that, nothing unusual happened, sir. She wore a double set of gloves for the next three hours. None of the seeds she handled with the double gloves show any signs of unusual growth. She did it herself somehow, and she knows it. Even more, she's learning to control it. Whatever this creature is that you had us adopt, it's beginning to become aware of what it is. I'll need some orders, sir, about how to proceed. I'm nervous about it being in the greenhouse with all of my biological warfare research. If it starts fiddling with the poisonous plants, who knows what might happen? What shall I do?"

The film cut off. General Meade sat back in his chair, rubbing his jaw. After a moment's thought, he retrieved a piece of paper from his case and wrote a short note:

"Let her continue in the greenhouse and monitor her progress closely. Try to keep her away from the poisonous plants. That's an experiment for another time. Keep me informed about her progress both with her special abilities as well as her education. She's young enough to mold into what we want and old enough that we won't have to wait for more than a couple of years for her to mature. She may be the best soldier of the lot, so take good care of her, and for God's sake, get your wife to warm up a little. This kid needs a mother, and if we give her one, she'll be entirely under our power."

Signing it, he folded the note and put it in an envelope, which he sealed then put inside another sealed envelope. He'd give that to the courier later today. In the meantime, he had to look through the latest UFO data. The activity seemed to be gaining pace, with increased sightings in the stratosphere and more low runs over sensitive military installations on all continents. He hoped they would have time to develop his new army before the invasion. If they didn't, everything would be lost.

Two hours later, he, Jones, and a Pentagon hypnotist sat in a windowless, soundproofed white room. Zion Wilson lay on a white recliner, his eyes fluttering in half-consciousness. Dr. Jones and the hypnotist sat behind him, and General Meade stood in front. Jones busied himself with examining Wilson's vital statistics from a machine hooked up to the patient while the hypnotist spoke in low, soothing tones, his voice never rising above a whisper and never stopping.

"You remember nothing. You are nothing. Your mind is a blank slate. Today you will become something new, and that will be the only thing you want to be. Your name is Orion. Orion. Orion. You are coming awake now. When you do, you will open your eyes. Standing before you is your master, General Meade. General Meade. General Meade. He is all that matters. You will obey him every day for the rest of your life. He is your life. You exist only to serve him..."

General Meade shifted nervously while he waited for the patient to wake up. This was the final test. He needed these Atlanteans to serve him and him alone. Only then could he be sure they would be used correctly. The future of the project was far too important to let his commanders in the Pentagon have a say in it. Doing this was far beyond his orders and counted as gross insubordination. Considering the patient's status as government property, it could even be considered theft. If the Pentagon brass heard of this, he'd be knocked down to private and be reassigned to cleaning latrines in Guantanamo until retirement.

But there was no other way. This was too important to trust with anyone else. Only Jones and the hypnotist, Dr. Bill Ziegler, knew what was happening here. Luckily they were both under his thumb. Jones was a weakling, and Meade had dug up enough on Ziegler's past to ensure his silence. He had told Ziegler that at the first sign of his disobedience, the world would discover that his title of "doctor" had been purchased from a fake university on the Internet. A second slipup would lead to Mrs. Ziegler getting some photos of her hypnotist husband and a certain young woman. Any further rebellion would be quashed by Marquis, who could get quite messy with an ice pick. He was even messier, and slower, with a sharpened spoon. Meade had seen the photos, and they were worse than anything he'd seen on the battle-field. Ziegler had thrown up when he saw them. The hypnotist would be no trouble at all.

Ziegler would behave, and despite his seedy secret life and fake degree, he was quite the hypnotist. When Meade had discovered him, he had been working for the mafia. Why the mafia needed a hypnotist was something Meade had never found out and wasn't sure he wanted to know. Mrs. Ziegler knew all about her husband's mob connections and didn't mind as long as the money kept rolling in.

Civilians. No wonder this country was going down the toilet.

Ziegler's voice purred on. "You will awaken soon, Orion. The first person you see will be General Meade, your master. Your life is his. You live to serve him. Now I will count backward to zero, and you will awaken. Ten… nine… eight…"

General Meade stood at attention in front of the recliner. This was the moment of truth. Of all the things he had done, this was the act that would finally mark his break with the armed forces. From now on, the country he'd sworn to protect could quite rightly consider him a maverick and a traitor, even though his actions were all guided by a sense of duty to his nation.

"Seven... six... five..."

More than four decades of service. Three public wars and a dozen secret ones. How many people had he killed to protect America? How many cities had he bombed? How many foreign politicians and scientists had he assassinated? It all seemed such a waste. He didn't feel any sympathy for America's enemies, but mankind should be united in the face of a far greater enemy. Race? Religion? Nationality? All meant nothing if an enemy was coming from the stars.

"Four... three... two..."

He'd done so many things out of necessity. Killed, maimed, burned, imprisoned, but he had never enslaved. Killing was natural, normal. Slavery, though, that was a sin. He had fought all his life to preserve freedom and felt there was no more terrible thing than to take it away from an innocent person.

And that was exactly what he was about to do here.

"One…"

There was no other way, General Meade kept telling himself. Enslave a few in order to save the rest. It was a terrible, necessary sacrifice.

"Awaken!"

General Meade tensed as Orion opened his eyes and looked right at him.

Stiffly, Orion got off the recliner and knelt before Meade. Though his voice croaked from lack of use, he said, "I am yours, General."

Meade slumped. Yes, a necessary sacrifice, but why was it always him forcing someone else to make the sacrifice?

# Chapter 16

JUNE 18, 2016, PRESBYTERIAN
HOSPITAL, ALBUQUERQUE, NEW
MEXICO

11:35 AM

Dr. Akiko Yamazaki lay in her hospital bed, struggling to understand. It was so difficult. The world felt muted, distant. Her thoughts were disorganized, and half the time, she couldn't remember basic things.

She knew she had suffered a stroke, and she knew it had happened in some strange circumstance. There was something menacing about her illness, as if it hadn't happened in the usual way, but she couldn't remember what. It was just a feeling. Her feelings also told her it had something to do with her job. She was a geneticist, one of the best in the world, and she had been studying... something.

Trying to organize her thoughts was exhausting, like trying to drink when the nurse came to feed her.

She slept.

Sometime later, she awoke with a new determination to come back to life. She struggled to move her arms and managed to move the right one an inch or so. At least she thought she had. She couldn't move her head to check.

So difficult. Maybe she should sleep again.

No. She had to keep trying.

She opened her eyes and stared at the white hospital ceiling. How long had she been here? Where had her assistant gone? He hadn't visited her in a while.

What was his name again? Yale? Yin?

Yuhle. That was it.

He was an astronomer like her.

No, wait, she was a geneticist. That meant Yuhle was an astronomer too.

No, a geneticist!

Dr. Yamazaki moaned. What horror. She had been brilliant once. Vaguely she remembered awards and conference invitations and papers in top journals. Now look at her, a mindless shell in a hospital bed.

Where was Yuhle? He had told her something important the last time he was there. What was it? Something about their project.

They were archaeologists, right? Something like that. And they were uncovering a lost civilization.

No, damn it. That was only half right. They were geneticists uncovering a lost civilization. Her boss's name was Ying. No, her assistant's name was Yuhle. They were geneticists, and they were uncovering a lost civilization.

How would a geneticist do that? She couldn't remember.

Tears welled out of her eyes. She'd never be the same again. If only Ying would come visit again. He could explain the archaeology project to her, and she'd understand.

Dr. Yamazaki sensed movement in the room. She blinked her tears away and looked toward the door. They had positioned her bed so she could see the door without having to move her head. That was kind. They were kind to the dead here.

Two people were looking through the door's window at her, talking in low tones.

"We've come to help, Dr. Yamazaki," a voice said close to her ear.

She turned her eyes and saw another two people standing by her bed. For a moment, confusion blurred her thoughts. She looked back at the door and saw two people there. Turning back, she saw two people at the side of her bed.

Were there two or four?

No, there were four. She just hadn't noticed them come in.

She sighed and closed her eyes. Her life was over. Why couldn't she just die and get it over with?

"Can you understand me, Dr. Yamazaki?" the voice asked.

She opened her eyes again. Two people in doctor's scrubs stood by the bed. They were both mixed race with bright blue eyes. Dr. Yamazaki looked toward the door. The other pair who stood there looked the same.

Black skin. Blue eyes. Asian features. That meant something. She used to know what.

Maybe Yuhle and Ying could explain it to her once they got back from the observatory.

"Dr. Yamazaki, I'm going to lay my hands on your head for a moment. Don't worry if you feel a strange sensation. It will help your condition. I need you to remain calm and quiet. Do you under-stand me?"

"I already had an injection." She heard her words come out as a mumble.

"What did she say?" the voice asked.

"It doesn't matter," a second voice replied. "Do your thing."

There was silence for a moment. She felt someone touching her head and a slight dizziness.

"Hurry up," the second voice whispered.

"It's done."

Dr. Yamazaki hadn't felt the injection. Had they given her one? She didn't feel pain anymore, only despair.

One of the figures bent over her. "Dr. Yamazaki, you will feel better very soon. There will be a period of disorientation and nausea. Don't worry, that's normal. It will take a couple of hours before you're completely better. In the meantime, please lie quietly. We're going to take you out of here. You're in danger."

Dr. Yamazaki felt confused. Take her out of the hospital? She was in danger?

Wait, yes, she was in danger. She couldn't remember why though. It probably had something to do with her assistant Yuhle and the genetics project.

"Where are you taking me?" she asked as she heard the clamps securing the wheels on her hospital bed being released. The two figures wheeled her bed toward the door.

"What was that?" one of them asked.

"Where are you taking me?" She tried to enunciate, and she heard her words come out clearer.

"You're getting better already. We're taking you someplace safe."

The hospital room doors opened, and they wheeled the bed into the hallway. Dr. Yamazaki turned her head and saw three people waiting in the hallway. Two of them were women. All of them, like the two who had taken her from her room, had the same strange mix of racial features.

What did that mean? She knew it was important.

They wheeled her down the hall, whispering among themselves and sounding nervous.

"Excuse me, where are you taking this patient?" demanded a stern woman's voice. Dr. Yamazaki thought she recognized the voice as her regular nurse's.

"We're taking her in for an EKG and a blood test."

"I wasn't informed."

Dr. Yamazaki turned her head and saw her regular nurse talking with one of the men who had come into her room.

The nurse looked at her, and her jaw dropped. "She turned her head! And her eyes are focusing as well. That's remarkable. She hasn't had this much improvement for weeks, if at all."

"Yes," the man said. "That's why we're taking her for tests."

The nurse studied him then turned to look at each of the strangers in turn. "Just who are you, anyway?"

"We have IDs."

"I can see that. The thing is, I've been working here for years, and I don't recognize you."

The man speaking to her jabbed a hypo into her neck. The nurse's eyes rolled up, and she slumped. He stopped her fall, shouldered open the nearest door, and dragged her inside. He reappeared a moment later, calling over his shoulder, "You just sleep for a while, lady, and by the time you wake up, we'll be long gone."

The strangers continued wheeling Dr. Yamazaki down the hallway. Her mind spun. What was going on?

They barely made it ten feet before there was a shout behind them.

"Hey!"

The sound of running feet.

Dr. Yamazaki turned her head and looked over her shoulder. The wave of nausea this movement produced kept her from wondering how she was able to do it at all.

Two burly men in black suits ran down the hallway toward them. They looked familiar. A flash of a memory of being pulled out of a classroom came to her, but she couldn't recall the time or place.

The two strangers at the back of the group turned to face the men in suits.

The newcomers stopped. One pulled an ID out of his pocket. "Federal agent. Stop what you're doing and get up against the wall!"

One of the doctors kicked him in the stomach. The agent doubled over and flew backward a couple of yards, landing hard on the tile floor. The other agent cursed and pulled out a semi-automatic pistol.

The second doctor lashed out with a karate chop to the second agent's wrist. There was a loud snap muffled by the gun going off. A bullet whined overhead and burst a fluorescent light on the ceiling, sending down a cascade of sparks and glass.

The doctors gave the agent a couple more punches, and he dropped to the floor, unconscious.

Yamazaki heard screams from down the hallway. An alarm sounded, wailing high and piercing in the echoing hallway.

"Damn it! Let's get out of here!" one of the doctors shouted.

"Where are you taking me?" Dr. Yamazaki demanded, struggling to get up.

A gentle yet firm hand pressed her back down on the mattress. "You just lie back and relax."

The doctors hurried her down the hallway. Nurses and visitors leapt out of their way. They turned a corner and came to an elevator. One of the doctors jabbed a button.

"Who are you?" Dr. Yamazaki asked.

"We've come to help, just like you tried to help us," one of them said.

"What?" she asked, confused. Her mind was still whirling. Even though her thoughts were becoming clearer by the minute, it was all going too fast. She didn't have time for her muddled mind to catch up.

The elevator door pinged open. The doctors hauled a couple of startled orderlies out of it and pushed her bed inside. Dr. Yamazaki raised her head again and looked out into the corridor. Just as the doors were closing, a pair of hospital security guards rounded the corner.

"There they are," one of them shouted, pointing.

The doors slid shut.

"Come on, come on," one of the doctors muttered impatiently, jabbing the ground floor button.

The elevator jerked to a stop.

"What did you do!" one of the doctors cried.

"Nothing, just hit the button!"

"It wasn't him. It was the security guards. They did a manual override. We're trapped!"

"Not for long," one of the female doctors said.

She clambered onto Dr. Yamazaki's bed and pushed on the ceiling. An emergency hatch wrenched free, the screws squealing and snapping. She hadn't even bothered to turn the handle.

Dr. Yamazaki's eyes widened. Strange features… super strength… she knew these people. They were what she'd been studying with Yuhle. What were they? Where were they from? She had to remember.

She didn't get the chance. The woman disappeared into the elevator shaft, followed by another. Then a third of these strange people lifted Dr. Yamazaki up into waiting hands.

Things grew dark as she was carried up the elevator shaft. The man who carried her held onto her with one hand and shimmied up the elevator cable with his other hand and two feet. Impossible!

But no, she had been studying these people because, as unbelievable as their powers were, they were all too real.

"Let's go up a couple of floors. They'll still be waiting at the door."

"So what? They don't have guns."

"The cops who will join them any second sure do."

"Right, we'll go up another floor and come down the stairs."

Dr. Yamazaki's stomach churned. Even the simplest movement of her head made her feel ill, and now she was being carried like a rag doll up a dark elevator shaft. She gagged and her breakfast came up, falling onto the man climbing below her.

"Oh, for God's sake!" he cried out.

The man carrying Dr. Yamazaki laughed. "You join the army, and you pay the price."

*Army? What army? Certainly not the US army, that's for sure.* She tried to voice the question and found she felt too weak. They probably wouldn't answer her anyway.

There was a screech of metal above her, followed by a flood of light and several screams. Dr. Yamazaki looked up, feeling her stomach quake again. The woman who had led them out of the elevator had pried open the elevator doors on a higher floor and was reaching down to grab her. As the woman lifted her into a hallway, the dribble of vomit on Dr. Yamazaki's chin smeared off on her shoulder.

"Sorry," she mumbled.

The woman looked at her ruined shirt with distaste then shrugged. "I've made bigger sacrifices than this."

They were surrounded by a half circle of astonished nurses and visitors who backed away as, one by one, more dark-skinned doctors with brilliant blue eyes climbed out of the elevator shaft.

"Let's move!" the woman holding Dr. Yamazaki barked. "The cops won't take long to figure out where we are."

They hurried down the hallway, the crowd parting before them. Dr. Yamazaki spotted a security camera and wondered if her abductors realized they had already been noticed.

The group burst into the stairway and hurried down. They rounded one floor then a second. As they came around another turn, there was a loud bang and the lead man staggered back, clutching his arm.

"I've been shot!"

Dr. Yamazaki caught a glimpse of a pair of blue uniforms in the stairwell below them before her group hurried back around the corner. Another shot pinged off the wall, the ricochet whining past her ear.

"Careful, you idiot!" someone shouted from below. "You might hit the hostage!"

It took a moment for Dr. Yamazaki to realize that the cop meant her. *Am I a hostage?* She clung to the woman carrying her. They certainly had taken her without her permission, but they were curing her too. She looked with amazement at her hands, once so useless and now holding on with a child's strength to the strange woman who had pulled her out of the elevator shaft.

The buzz of a radio echoed up the stairwell as the police called for backup. The doctors huddled against the wall, out of sight from the police below.

"What do we do?" the woman carrying her asked.

"Break through," replied the man who had been shot. He was still gripping his arm, blood trickling through his fingers, but otherwise he looked remarkably unhurt.

"How?" one of the others asked.

The man who was shot inclined his head and hurried up the stairs to the next floor. Curious, the others followed. He opened the door, peeked through, and slammed it without going through.

"No one there yet," he whispered. "Guard this door. I'll clear the way below."

Dr. Yamazaki heard the police whispering on the floor below, then she heard stealthy steps on the stairs. The shot man nodded to his companions and walked down the stairs.

"I give up!" he called. "Don't shoot!"

He rounded the corner, raising his one good arm.

"Hold it right there, buddy!" one of the cops ordered.

"The others ran off upstairs. I don't have the strength to go with them. I surrender!"

"On your knees!"

"Don't shoot! I'll tell you everything!"

There was a thud and a groan, followed an instant later by a shot and a loud crash, then the sound of a body tumbling down the stairs.

"The way's clear," the doctor called up. His voice sounded strained.

They hurried down, Dr. Yamazaki feeling ill as she bounced along in the woman's arms. The strange woman didn't seem any more tired from running around with her than if she had been holding a bag of groceries. As they rounded the corner, Dr. Yamazaki saw the doctor leaning against the wall, clutching his side. One cop lay groaning at his feet. The other was sprawled on the landing several steps down.

"You've been hit again!" one of the other doctors exclaimed.

"Thanks for stating the obvious." The wounded man grinned. "I'll live, but you're going to have to carry me."

One of the doctors hauled him up onto his shoulders, and they stepped over the policemen.

"You didn't kill them, did you?"

"Of course not. Not that I wasn't tempted. The bastards shot me twice."

"We should have planned this better," the woman carrying Dr. Yamazaki muttered. "Some army this is. What a joke."

They hurried down to the bottom level and burst out into an underground garage. Dr. Yamazaki looked around and breathed a sigh of relief when she saw no one. While she still didn't know what was going on, she was placing her bets on her abductors. Those federal agents upstairs were her enemies—somehow she knew that—and while the police and hospital security were only doing their jobs, they would hand her over to the federal government, then she'd be lost forever.

The last person in line peered up the stairwell then hurried back and shut the door. "They're coming. Get in the van." He bent the metal door handle until it twisted off with a loud snap.

Everyone ran across the garage to a van marked *Industrial Plumbing, Ltd*. They opened the back and hurried inside. Dr. Yamazaki was placed on a cot, and the others shucked off their medical scrubs and replaced them with workman's overalls. The wounded man had to be helped into his. While he looked pale and in pain, Yamazaki noted that his bleeding had stopped.

"Who are you people?" she asked as someone put a trench coat on over her hospital robe.

"We'll explain everything if we survive the next five minutes," someone said.

The woman who had carried her put shoes on Dr. Yamazaki's feet. Another woman got into the driver's seat and backed the van out.

Ignoring the nausea that pulled at her stomach, Dr. Yamazaki struggled to sit up and looked through the windshield between the driver's and passenger seat. They were driving up the ramp toward the exit. Bright sunlight made her blink. By the entrance stood a little security box and a red-and-white-striped traffic barrier.

"Got your parking permit?" the wounded man joked.

"No time for that." The driver laughed, slamming on the gas.

They smashed through the barrier and peeled out onto the street. Dr. Yamazaki's head spun, and she threw up again, most of it ending up in the cup holder between the seats. Someone tried to push her back onto the cot, but she batted the hand away. She had to see what was going on. The van swung into traffic.

"No cops in sight. I think we lost them," the driver said.

"They'll be on us soon enough," one of the others replied.

They continued driving, zigzagging down back streets and into a residential district in the hope of eluding pursuit. Dr. Yamazaki had enough time to clear her thoughts a little.

Atlanteans. These people carried the Atlantis gene. She had been studying them for the government, heading a secret project called… something… headed by a General… Mitchell? No, that wasn't it.

"Damn it, why can't I remember?" she cried, slamming her fist against the seat in front of her.

"It will come with time," one man said.

She was about to ask what he had done to her when another voice made everyone turn.

"Hey, that car has been following us for a while."

That came from the wounded man, who was sitting up again and looking out the back window. Dr. Yamazaki saw a black sedan tailing them from a discreet distance. The van screeched to a halt, and Dr. Yamazaki was thrown between the driver's and passenger seats.

And that saved her life.

A burst of machine gun fire smashed through the windshield. The pair in the front two seats jerked as bullets tore through their bodies. A heavy weight fell on her as one of the Atlanteans sitting beside her took a bullet to the head.

There was a loud crash, and the van rocked from side to side. Dr. Yamazaki stared wide-eyed as two of the surviving Atlanteans kicked the side of the van, buckling and finally tearing through the metal. Within moments, a huge hole yawned where there had been a solid wall of steel. One of them grabbed her, and they leapt outside.

In front of the van, a black sedan sat across the two-lane residential road. Two men with machine guns were pouring fire into the van. Behind the van, the sedan that had been following them had blocked off the road as well, and two agents were emerging from the car.

One of the Atlanteans leapt a full ten feet to crash into the driver of the rear car as he got out of the vehicle. The man fell hard to the pavement and did not rise. The Atlantean leapt over the car at the other agent, who pulled out a pistol and fired twice before getting knocked down.

The man holding Dr. Yamazaki sprinted for the car. Dr. Yamazaki looked back at the agents wielding machine guns just in time to see them aim at them.

"Look out!" she screamed.

Too late. A burst of gunfire hit the Atlantean in the back. He hugged Dr. Yamazaki close to shield her and staggered to the car. His comrade had already gotten inside and gunned the engine. Dr. Yamazaki was tossed in the backseat, and she cowered as the car screeched in a U-turn and peeled down the road.

Bullets smashed through the rear window, and the sedan swerved, straightened out, and picked up speed.

Dr. Yamazaki dared to peek into the front seat. The driver leaned hard against the door, blood pouring from several wounds. The passenger seat was empty. The man who had saved her from the van hadn't made it into the car.

She scrambled into the front. The Atlantean at the wheel gave her a bleary-eyed look that told her he was struggling to stay conscious.

Movement in the rearview mirror caught her eye. The other sedan was after them and gaining fast. She found their own car slowing down, the Atlantean's foot sliding off the gas as he slumped in his seat.

The car rocked as the pursuing sedan slammed into their rear fender.

A turn was coming up. Dr. Yamazaki grabbed the wheel and yanked it hard to the right, tires squealing as she managed to make the turn and even out.

The other sedan wasn't so lucky. Eager to ram them off the road, the agents hadn't been looking at the path ahead. They smashed right through a fire hydrant, a fence, and straight into the brick wall of a house.

Dr. Yamazaki gripped the steering wheel tightly as the vehicle gradually lost speed. With one hand, she felt for the Atlantean's pulse and found none. As the car bumped to a stop on the curb, she eased him out of the driver's seat and took his place.

She soon found she wasn't coordinated enough yet to drive. She zigzagged for a couple of miles in the back streets of the residential neighborhood, getting honked at several times for cutting people off or running stop signs before she finally gave up. The car was riddled with bullet holes, and someone must have called the police by now. While they wouldn't shoot her on sight like those agents, they'd take her into custody. Then she would be dead sooner or later.

Before she abandoned the vehicle, she rifled through the Atlantean's pockets, taking a wallet, a phone, and a small can of pepper spray. Guilt tugged at her for robbing a man who had given his life to save her, but this was survival. He would want her to take anything that might help her elude capture.

Stumbling out of the car, she hobbled away, trying to get her rubbery legs to move her along. She cut through parks and backyards as startled faces stared at her through windows. In the distance she heard the *chop chop chop* of a police helicopter approaching.

# Chapter 17

JUNE 18, 2016, ALBUQUERQUE, NEW MEXICO

2:07 PM

Orion had proved to be a better candidate than expected. Who would have thought a mild-mannered nobody from civilian life could turn into a super soldier with less than a day's training?

Yet that's what had happened.

Orion stood in a special training room, much like the one Marquis D'Arcy had created for Jaxon. A line of weights were stacked on a rack to one side. In a corner hung an especially durable punching bag. Wooden dummies used for kung-fu stood to one side of the room.

Orion was working through those right now. He gave a blindingly fast round-house kick to one, sending it spinning on its moveable stand, then he punched the next one low in the stomach. He leapt up and planted two side kicks to the heads of the next dummies, and continued on.

General Meade watched in awe and more than a little fear. Imagine what such a soldier could do in the wrong hands!

Every hit was directly on a pressure point, marked by a network of black dots on the bodies of the dummies, and every hit was incredibly powerful. If the dummies hadn't been specially designed to take a massive amount of punishment, they would have already shattered into splinters. This guy could hit like a black belt, and as far as General Meade knew, he hadn't had any military training before today.

General Meade was training Orion himself. He wished he could bring in Marquis, but he was doing more valuable work with Jaxon. A willing servant was far more valuable than this slave. It would be nice if Meade could bring in one of the other martial arts instructors the military could supply, but he knew better than to ask the Pentagon for more funding.

At least not yet. Once they saw how well Orion was doing, they'd cough up the funds quickly enough.

And Orion was amazing. The general had given the Atlantean a basic, first-day course in kung-fu and shown him some videos of some traditional masters from the Shaolin temple, then he'd left Orion to figure out the rest himself. Now he was performing better than Meade ever could, despite his years of martial arts training and practice. Give Orion a few more days, and he'd give Marquis a run for his money.

Dr. Jones stood to one side with a clipboard, making notes. After Orion went through a few more moves with the martial arts dummies, the scientist asked him to lift some weights. Orion went over to the bench press, where Dr. Jones had prepared a bar with three hundred sixty pounds, twice Orion's body weight.

"Do as many bench presses as you can," Dr. Jones said.

Orion looked at General Meade, who nodded.

*He doesn't have any will beyond what I say, does he?* The general felt a twinge of guilt. *I've become a slave master.*

He thought of his great-great-grand-father, who had been a colonel in the Union army in the Civil War. Old Phineas Meade, a cousin of the more famous General Meade of that time, had been an abolitionist, fighting in the South to free the slaves.

General Meade had always been proud of his Civil War heritage, both the famous general who had won Gettysburg and the lesser-known colonel who had been a minister in civilian life, preaching against the evils of slavery before exchanging his frock for a uniform in order to put those beliefs into practice.

And there he was, one hundred fifty years later, sullying their memory by becoming a slave owner.

*It's necessary*, he repeated to himself. *It's necessary.*

Orion lay on the padded bench and gripped the bar. He pulled it off its metal hooks and did a smooth, effortless bench press. The sight of this unassuming man bench pressing three hundred sixty pounds brought General Meade out of his thoughts. He'd seen Marines twice Orion's size incapable of doing that.

Orion pulled the bar to his chest and lifted it again. He did it ten more times before his face turned red, and he slammed the bar back on the hooks.

"He just did a set of twelve bench presses at twice his body weight, and we haven't even started him on his workout routine!" Dr. Jones exclaimed.

"Make a note of everything," General Meade ordered. "This will get us more funding, including a trainer for him and an assistant for you." *Or perhaps a replacement for you.*

Dr. Jones nodded eagerly and instructed Orion to move to the pull-up bar. Once again Orion looked to the general for confirmation, and once again Meade felt that twinge of guilt.

"Do whatever Dr. Jones asks unless I say otherwise," General Meade said.

Orion nodded and went over to the bar, where he went through a smooth series of pull-ups in rapid succession.

General Meade's cell phone rang in his pocket. Grumbling with frustration, he turned away and answered. "What is it?"

"It's Agent Kelly, sir. There's a problem."

"Well, spit it out, agent."

As Agent Kelly told him about the Atlanteans sneaking into Presbyterian Hospital dressed as doctors, subduing Dr. Yamazaki's guards, and abducting her, General Meade felt a chill. As the agent went on to describe the fight with the police, the car chase, and Dr. Yamazaki's escape, that chill turned into something close to terror.

General Meade knew all about fear. There was nothing wrong with a soldier being afraid. Anyone who wasn't afraid in the middle of a battle was a psycho, and psychos posed as much danger to their own side as the enemy's. So while he accepted his fear, he never liked it. It meant he wasn't in control of the situation.

"So wait, you mean to tell me Dr. Yamazaki *ran away*?"

"Well, drove away, sir. The vehicle was found a couple of miles away, and she wasn't in it. She appears to have escaped on foot."

"Yesterday she couldn't even move her foot," General Meade said.

There was a long pause.

"I have no explanation, sir."

"And the Atlanteans?"

"Four dead, the other two captured."

"Bring them here," Meade said.

"The local police are asking a lot of questions about—"

"Bring them here!"

"Yes, sir."

"And put a news blackout on the whole thing. National security. The cops will toe the line. And think of some cover story."

Kelly said, "Sir, there was a newspaper reporter in the hospital covering an unrelated story when the shooting broke out. We have him in custody."

"Call Agent Lewis Frederickson at the local DEA office. He's one of ours. I'll send you his number. Ask him to get some crystal meth out of the evidence locker and give it to you. Plant it on this reporter, find it, and threaten him with arrest if he doesn't keep his mouth shut."

"Yes, sir."

General Meade nodded with approval. Agent Kelly wasn't the quickest or most original thinker on the payroll, but he followed orders without question. "And find Dr. Yamazaki. No, wait. Locate and tail her. It'll be interesting to see where she goes. Report back to me hourly."

"Yes, sir."

The agent hung up. General Meade stared at his phone, wishing he could disbelieve what he had just heard. He turned to Orion. "Come over here."

The Atlantean hurried over like some eager dog. Dr. Jones followed with a curious expression.

"So tell me, Orion, have you met any others of your kind?" General Meade asked.

Orion stared at him for a moment, looked at Dr. Jones, then slowly surveyed the room. "No."

"I mean before you came here," the general asked.

Orion looked confused. "Before?"

Dr. Jones cleared his throat. "Um, sir, you're forgetting the drug."

General Meade sighed. How foolish of him. Orion was, at least mentally, in his first days of life. Whatever he had experienced before had been wiped away and would stay that way, at least as long as they kept giving him the memory suppressant.

"Go back to your training, Orion. Jones, stay here for a minute." Once Orion was out of earshot and working out with some ridiculously heavy weights, General Meade said in a low voice, "I want you to wake up another of the subjects. Pick the oldest."

"That would be Emma Blankenship. She's fifty-three," the scientist replied.

"Good. She'll have had plenty of time to meet others of her kind. Maybe she'll have some information she can tell us. Use that truth serum I supplied you with."

A few hours later, Dr. Jones and General Meade stood on either side of an examination table in the laboratory. On it lay Emma Blankenship. As with Orion, it had taken Dr. Jones some time to bring her out of hibernation and prepare her to wake up. In that time, as per orders, Agent Kelly had called in hourly reports.

Those reports were not encouraging. They hadn't managed to track down Dr. Yamazaki, and the captive Atlanteans were not talking. That was annoying but not disastrous. With time they'd find the runaway scientist, and Meade could make those genetic freaks spill the beans.

Getting some prisoners was the first real victory they'd had in this war. Not only did he have the aliens to contend with, but now it appeared there really was a group of Atlantean terrorists. The information he could extract would be priceless. That didn't mean what he and this mediocre scientist were doing now was a waste of time. Gathering as much intelligence as possible always paid off in a war. Different individuals could provide different clues as to what was going on.

"She's waking up," Dr. Jones said. "The truth serum should have kicked in by now. You can ask her anything you like."

Emma Blankenship's eyes fluttered open. "Whaaaa?"

"Welcome back, Ms. Blankenship. Can you understand me?"

The Atlantean turned her head and looked at Meade through puffy eyes. She looked as if she had just woken up and desperately needed some coffee.

"Ms. Blankenship, have you ever met more of your kind?"

She focused on him. Even though some clarity came to her eyes, she still seemed half asleep, a product of the truth serum. "More people like me? For so long I thought I was alone. I was put up for adoption as an infant and was always different. It was so lonely. It seemed like I could never fit in. My foster parents were kind enough, and I didn't move around like a lot of kids in the system, but I always felt apart from everyone else, like there was some invisible wall separating me from them."

General Meade stifled his impatience. His entire project was in danger from all angles, and this woman was telling him her life story. The details might be important though, so he didn't interrupt.

The Atlantean went on. "Things got stranger when I became a teenager.

Maybe puberty set it off—I don't know. I had always been athletic, but my strength and speed increased to something beyond human. I hid it as much as I could because I was always the odd one out. I didn't want to be rejected even more." Tears welled out of her eyes.

She wiped them and continued. "Then something truly remarkable happened. When I was fourteen, I started hearing voices. It was like background chatter, and there was music too. I thought I was going insane until I recognized one of the voices as that of a local DJ. The voices came from all the city radio stations. After a time, I learned how to focus my thoughts to tune into particular frequencies. I also learned to dampen them out so I could get some peace. My range increased, and now my head is a better receiver than the most expensive radio on the market."

General Meade rubbed his jaw. That was a useful ability. This woman had potential.

"These abilities made me feel even more alone. Eventually I came to terms with it. I never had many friends, never got married, and resigned myself to always being the odd person out. Until a few months ago."

"What happened?" the general asked.

"I met a guy at a bar. Sometimes I'm so lonely I go pick up men. A bit pathetic, I know, but there are times when you just need to be with someone. This guy was different. He looked a lot like me. Mixed race, or at least that's what I used to think. We got to talking and moved to a booth near the back for a little more privacy. Once we were out of sight, he took a spoon and bent it with just two fingers. I couldn't believe it. He was more like me than I had hoped! Then he told me that he was part of a group of similar people. They'd found each other by chance and were searching for more like themselves."

General Meade bent over her. "Did he say where they were based? How many there are? What's their group called?"

Emma shook her head. "I don't know. Just as he was telling me all of this, he got a kind of distant look in his eye, like he was listening to something I couldn't hear. I suppose I look like that when I'm listening to radio broadcasts in my head. There weren't any strange radio signals though. I checked. Suddenly he looked nervous and said he had to go. He asked for my address and said he'd be in touch. But he never got back to me. A couple of weeks later, I ended up here."

The general thought for a moment. "Work with Dr. Jones to make a sketch of this fellow. Provide any details you can remember about him, no matter how unimportant they may seem to you."

He turned away, his mind racing. That group of Atlanteans had almost taken Ms. Blankenship before they got her. Did they know of the Poseidon Project? And why had that Atlantean suddenly run off?

General Meade's phone rang again. He walked to the far end of the lab to answer it without being overheard.

"Agent Kelly reporting in, sir."

"I can see that from my screen, agent. Any news?"

"Yes, sir, actually we have some excellent news..."

# Chapter 18

JUNE 18, 2016, MOJAVE DESERT, NEVADA

10:30 PM

Otto could get used to the idea of being a freedom fighter. Of course, he didn't quite know what he was fighting against, and neither did his comrades-in-arms, but it sure beat cleaning up other people's trash by the side of the highway while wearing an orange jumpsuit.

As weird as the other people in the Atlantis Allegiance were, he really liked them. They had a goal, and they banded together like a bizarre little family. Otto had never had goals or a family. He wondered if his parents even cared that he had busted out of jail. Probably not, unless they were using it as ammunition against each other in one of their endless arguments.

Of course he was worried—worried about the government finding him and the rest of the Atlantis Allegiance, worried about Jaxon, worried that the Four Rottweilers of the Apocalypse might tear him apart and have him for dinner when Grunt wasn't looking—yet he found this new life thrilling.

At the moment, he stood beside Yuhle and Grunt behind the trailers. The shooting range was illuminated by a bright floodlight on top of one of the trailers, and a pair of man-sized targets stood not far off.

"Okay, maggots," Grunt said in a voice that reminded Otto of every drill instructor in every war movie he had ever seen, "today we're going to train you in the use of the Taser, the leading electrical weapon in the world. What's good about Tasers over stun guns is that they don't just hurt. If you're fighting someone tough enough, or psycho enough, pain won't be enough to stop them. It might just piss them off instead. But the Taser packs enough voltage to cause muscle contractions. Whoever you hit will be flopping around on the ground like a fish out of water no matter how tough they are."

Grunt handed Yuhle and Otto each a large black-and-yellow Taser. They looked like oversized toy pistols with a pair of metal spikes on the end. Nevertheless, Otto held his gingerly, not wanting to zap himself. Yuhle took a stance that he probably thought made him look cool, adjusted his glasses, and aimed at the targets Grunt had set up at a distance.

"Easy there, Tex," Grunt said.

"I already know how to handle a gun," Yuhle said with a cocky air.

"Okay then, hombre, give it your best shot," Grunt said.

Yuhle aimed, adjusted his glasses again, and pulled the trigger.

Nothing happened.

Grunt laughed. "If you were as good with a gun as you think you are, you'd have checked to see if the Taser has a safety. Spoiler alert! It does."

Yuhle blushed.

Grunt went on with his lecture. "The Taser uses a compressed nitrogen charge to fire a pair of electrodes. Those are inside the cartridges, which we have more of over here. Don't touch them. You probably want to point that away from you, Yuhle. Yes, and away from Otto too. Anyway, they're attached to the Taser by thin wires and can shoot up to thirty-five feet on these models. The electrodes are barbed so they stick through clothing into skin. Once they hit, they deliver a hefty electric charge. Your opponent will be down for the count. Now, these used to be one-shot weapons. No problem if you have good aim and are only dealing with one bad guy. With you two jokers, I think it's safe to say that's not the case. Luckily these are the latest model, the X3, and they can fire three shots before reloading. So you can take out three opponents without causing them any real harm."

Otto had noticed, to his relief, that he was only being trained to use nonlethal weapons. Killing Nazis or zombies in a videogame was one thing, but he didn't want to kill real people. From what Edward had said though, a lot of people in power wanted to kill Otto just for standing up to the government.

He wished he understood what was going on. He knew Jaxon was in danger, he knew he had been framed for a crime he didn't commit, and he knew that pretty much everything he thought he knew about the world was wrong. Other than that, he didn't know anything.

Grunt snapped his fingers in front of Otto's eyes. "Hey, pyro, wake up. This is important."

Otto focused again. Grunt went through the firing sequence then stood back to let them aim and shoot at their targets. Otto hit his, and Yuhle missed. They fired their next two shots, and Otto hit once more, as did Yuhle. Otto was relieved the scientist hadn't had to use his pistol during the prison break.

"Okay, maggots, reload. And shoot straight this time. Your lives might depend on it."

"I'm thinking a gun is better for what we're up against," Yuhle said, regaining his swagger.

"You might be right, professor, but I think you look much cuter with all ten of your toes. Reload and do it again," Grunt snapped.

Otto chuckled.

"Quiet, pyro. You only hit twice out of three times. That means one of your opponents got a chance to gut you."

"Ah... right," Otto said, turning off his Taser.

Vivian came strolling up. "How are the newbies, Grunt?"

"Terrible. Swagger like Rambo and fight like Teletubbies."

Vivian laughed.

"Aren't you guys supposed to do the fighting?" Otto said.

"If we get attacked, honey, we all have to fight." Vivian turned to Yuhle and held up a cell phone. "Your phone rang."

Yuhle's jaw dropped. "What? It's not even on. We agreed on that."

Vivian looked at Otto. "Cell phones can be tracked, so we keep our personal phones off. Since Yuhle dropped out of circulation, he shouldn't even be getting any calls, but he has."

"How do you know I got a call if my phone is off?" Yuhle asked. "Oh, wait. Edward?"

Vivian nodded. "Yeah, he tapped your phone account. It's actually not a call, but an email to one of the anonymous accounts you made at the Albuquerque Public Library before you left the Poseidon Project."

"Which one?" Yuhle asked. "And no, I don't need to know how you know about them."

"No secrets with Edward." Vivian chuckled. "It was an email to studmuffin@torguard.net."

Grunt cackled and slapped his knee. "Studmuffin? Well, they'll never suspect it's you!"

Yuhle ignored him. The scientist looked worried. "That account was just for Dr. Yamazaki and me. No one else knew about it."

Everyone fell silent. Yuhle had told them the story of his old boss and how she had suffered a mysterious stroke that Yuhle suspected had been inflicted on her somehow by General Meade. From what he had said, there was no way Dr.

Yamazaki could be up and using her email.

"Let's go see Edward," Yuhle said.

They found him where he always was—in his trailer in front of his computer screens. His shortwave radio wasn't on. Briefly Otto wondered if anyone would replace that earnest Spanish voice he had heard on his first visit.

Edward looked up from his computer screens. One showed a schematic of a disk-shaped machine with writing in German and a swastika beside the writing. Another looked like a topographic map of a portion of the ocean floor. The third computer screen had a short video running on a loop that showed a secret service man standing next to the president. The camera focused on the secret service man as his face slowly changed into something reptilian.

Otto shook his head. "Lizard aliens, Edward? Really?"

Edward held up a finger. "Not lizard aliens, but the conspiracy to get us to believe in lizard aliens."

"Ah... right."

Yuhle butted in. "What's this about me getting an email on one of my secret accounts?"

"Not too secret. I'm going to have to teach you about Internet security," Edward said.

"Whatever," the scientist replied, looking annoyed. "Can you open it safely?"

"Yeah, I can hack into it via the Tor network. My proxy server works through a proxy server. We won't be traced."

"Do it."

"Okay, studmuffin," Edward said with a grin.

Grunt cackled again. Edward's fingers danced over the center keyboard, and an inbox appeared on the central screen. It contained only one message with no subject line. Edward clicked on it.

The message contained only two words—"Subaru three."

Everyone gasped.

Everyone, that is, except Otto. "Subaru three? What does that mean?"

Edward ignored him and turned to Yuhle. "This was a code between you and Dr. Yamazaki?"

Yuhle nodded.

"What the hell does it mean?" Otto demanded.

"Ever noticed that all of our vehicles are Subarus, except for the Hummer?" Yuhle asked him.

"Um, yeah. So?"

"Subaru means Pleiades in Japanese," the scientist explained. "They're a cluster of bright blue stars in the constellation Orion. In Greek mythology, they're the daughters of Poseidon."

"You've lost me," Otto said.

"Poseidon was the god of the sea and the patron deity of Atlantis," Grunt said.

Otto looked at him in surprise.

Grunt shrugged. "I don't kill people and blow stuff up all the time. I get time to crack a book."

Otto bit his lip and looked back at the computer screen. "So couldn't this General Meade guy have gotten the code word and the email address from your old boss?"

Yuhle shook his head sadly. "Dr. Yamazaki couldn't even speak coherently when I last saw her. There's no way she's recovered enough for General Meade to have gotten that information out of her."

"They couldn't have even read her mind if the stroke was that bad because she wouldn't have remembered that information herself," Edward said.

"Reading minds? Come on, Edward, this is serious," Otto objected.

"And so am I. ESP exists, but the US army doesn't have any espers. Only the Swiss army does."

Otto turned away from the computer hacker. He didn't even want to hear the explanation on that one.

"So what does the 'three' mean?" Otto asked Yuhle.

The scientist adjusted his glasses. "It's one of our safe rendezvous points. When we decided to get out of the Poseidon Project, we went to a public library on separate days and set up anonymous email accounts. Verbally we agreed on a number code for several meeting points so if we were separated and in danger, we could meet. Number three is a diner in downtown Albuquerque. We set times to meet: ten in the morning and seven at night. She'll be there at both of those times until we go pick her up."

"This is a trap," Grunt said.

"We had a code to put in if we were emailing under duress," Yuhle said.

Grunt shook his head, the tribal tattoo on his face rippling in the dim light of the computer screen. "I don't care. Distress codes are standard procedure. If they were smart, they would have figured you'd agreed on one and tortured that information out of her too. This is a trap."

"Not necessarily," Vivian replied. "The real mystery is how she's recovered so quickly. Even if they cured her somehow and are holding her, we've got to try to get her free." She turned to Otto. "Looks like you got your first mission, honey."

"Me? I'm not a mercenary!"

"You're the only one she doesn't know, honey. Edward took one of her classes in college. Me and Grunt met her through Yuhle when he first got the idea of making the Atlantis Allegiance. Only you can get in close without her alerting her captors. And if she isn't captured, you can still check out the situation before we move in."

"What if I'm arrested for breaking out of prison?" Otto asked.

"We'll conceal your identity." Vivian smiled. "Makeover."

Otto let out a long, low sigh. He didn't see any way out of it. "All right, I'll do it."

***

At sunrise the following morning, they made it into Albuquerque. Otto was worn out from the eleven-hour drive. He hadn't been able to sleep much in the backseat as Vivian and Yuhle took turns driving. He had never been able to sleep well in cars, and the thought of stealing a scientist from under the noses of the federal government didn't exactly help.

Dawn broke clear behind them, silhouetting the New Mexican hills and sending golden rays over the desert. They stopped for breakfast at a waffle joint, then they idled in a park for a time, waiting for the ten o'clock rendezvous. Otto studied a map Edward had printed out of the streets around the diner.

"Make sure to memorize that, honey, because we have to destroy it," Vivian said.

She didn't look the least bit tired from her all-night drive from Nevada. Otto supposed she was used to this sort of thing. Yuhle, on the other hand, looked wrecked.

"Destroy it? Why?" Otto asked.

"Evidence," Yuhle said. "Never leave a paper trail. That's why I'm still alive."

Otto felt his heart flutter. As ten o'clock approached, Vivian fitted him with a small microphone and an ear plug so tiny and well camouflaged that Otto could barely see it when he looked in the Subaru's rearview mirror. The microphone was invisible too, hidden under his shirt.

"I'm going to be watching you through a sniper's scope, honey," Vivian said. "I'll tell you what to do. You just act natural as you do it."

"A sniper's scope? Is that going to be attached to a sniper's rifle?" Otto asked.

Vivian gave him a grin that would have looked more at home on Grunt's face.

Half an hour later, Otto strolled down a busy sidewalk, past morning commuters hurrying along to their office jobs. Cars honked in the heavy traffic of the street. So many people. Ever since his jailbreak, he'd been in the middle of the desert. He'd gotten used to the silence. A police car drove by. Otto tensed.

"He's on his regular rounds, honey," a sultry voice whispered in his ear, "and there's no radio chatter about you. Keep going."

"You people know everything," he whispered.

"The government knows more. Only talk if it's absolutely necessary."

Otto glanced at the nearby rooftops. Was Vivian up there somewhere? She hadn't told him from where she would be watching so that he couldn't inadvertently give her away. Otto forced himself to look straight ahead and act casual.

The diner was up ahead. It was one of those fake retro places that looked like an imitation of something from the old days of Route 66. A bright red neon sign flashed the words "Dan's Dandy Diner" over a sleek exterior that was almost entirely covered in chrome. Otto thought it looked like a toaster. Through the large windows, he saw people hunched over their late breakfasts, some in chattering groups and others sitting alone with their phones or laptops.

With his first glance through the window, Otto didn't spot Dr. Yamazaki, whose features he had memorized from a photo Yuhle had showed him. He went inside and scanned the interior. He saw a lone woman. She had long black hair and wore a trench coat. Otto casually walked between the booths, passed her without looking, and sat at an empty booth where he could get a better look at her.

It was Dr. Yamazaki. She looked thinner than in the photo Yuhle had shown him, and she was dressed oddly—in a man's trench coat over an old dress that looked as if it probably cost five dollars in a charity shop— but it was definitely her.

Otto pretended to look at the menu and tried to relax. His heart pounded. *She doesn't know you, so she can't give you away. You don't even know if this is a trap or not. Maybe she's not out to get you. But what about everyone else? That prison break, and your face, must have been all over the news.*

Vivian had thought of that and dyed his hair and put a bit of makeup on him to change his skin color. That felt woefully inadequate. Otto imagined all eyes were on him. He looked toward the front counter and saw the manager talking on a cell phone and looking in his direction.

*Don't be paranoid. If you look nervous, you could mess this whole thing up.*

He glanced at Dr. Yamazaki. She was hunched over a steaming cup of coffee and a Danish. She looked exhausted, deep lines of strain marking her face. She kept glancing out the window.

*Is she signaling someone? Waiting for the cops? Relax. She's waiting for Yuhle and is acting like anyone else who's waiting for someone. Chill out.*

A waitress strolled down to his booth. "What are you having, kid?"

"Do you have eggs Benedict?"

That was their agreed-on code to signal Vivian and Yuhle that he had spotted Dr. Yamazaki.

"Only what's on the menu, kid," the waitress said, sounding bored.

Otto's mind raced. If this was a trap, wouldn't she be nervous? Unless she was a cop or government agent who did this all the time. *Stop second-guessing yourself.*

"So what do you want?" the waitress asked.

"Um, just a Coke for now. Thanks."

The waitress nodded and walked off. Otto glanced around. The manager was no longer looking at him, and he didn't catch anyone else doing so either. So now what? Tell them the coast was clear? They had a code for that too.

"This place isn't bad," he mumbled.

Vivian's response came whispering into his ear. "Looks good out here too. Make your move, honey."

Summoning his courage, he stood and walked over to Dr. Yamazaki's booth. Her eyes widened as he sat down opposite her. She looked about to bolt.

"The Subaru is my favorite kind of car," he said. "How about yours?"

Dr. Yamazaki studied him, looking equal parts hopeful and suspicious. "Who are you?" she asked in a low voice.

"One of Yuhle's friends," he whispered and tensed. Now he had given himself away. At any moment a SWAT team might come busting in, throw him on the floor, cuff him, and haul him off to jail.

Dr. Yamazaki studied him. "Prove it."

Otto leaned in closer. "You and he formed the Atlantis Allegiance. You set up those anonymous email accounts in the public library. On his second day on the job, you nagged at him for being half an hour late. Anyone else know that stuff?"

A smile tugged at the corners of her lips. "I wouldn't say I 'nagged' at him."

"He would. He says you're testy about punctuality. Oh, and your favorite ice cream flavor is mint chocolate chip."

Dr. Yamazaki looked relieved. "Let's get out of here."

Just then the waitress came with his Coke. So as not to look suspicious, he ordered a bowl of cereal and spent a tense couple of minutes drinking his Coke.

Otto looked around to make sure no one else was sitting close enough to listen in. "The big bald guy with the ugly tattoo wants to know how you got away. And why you're vertical. He's the suspicious sort."

Dr. Yamazaki looked into her coffee. "I'm not sure myself. I was lying in the hospital when some of... *them* showed up."

"Our them or their them?"

Dr. Yamazaki smiled. "Our them."

Otto sat back, trying to hide his surprise. By the way she said it, she meant people like Jaxon. So there really were more of them.

Dr. Yamazaki went on. "One of them laid his hands on my head, and I got better within minutes. I was still too weak to move on my own, and while they were taking me out of the hospital, all hell broke loose. Federal agents, hospital security, the police, everything. The security and police seemed to be just trying to arrest us. I suppose they thought I was being kidnapped. The agents though"—she shuddered—"they gunned us down as fast as they could. I'm not sure any of the team that saved me survived."

Otto tensed. If they would do that to other Atlanteans, they would kill Jaxon just as quickly if she got out of line.

"But you got away," Otto said. That seemed too convenient. He knew Grunt would sure feel that way.

"Barely. One of them shielded me with his body. They managed to kill or incapacitate all the agents chasing me, but by then my new friends were all dead or dying." Dr. Yamazaki shuddered and wiped a tear from her eye. "What was strange was that none of them carried any guns. It was like they didn't want to kill anyone, not even the government agents. They weren't very well prepared. After that, I took a phone from one of them and his wallet. I hitchhiked everywhere. There was enough to get me a cheap motel, some clothes at Goodwill, and some food. I used the phone to email our mutual friend, then I waited for you to come."

Otto thought for a moment. What she said could be true. On the other hand, they hadn't heard a thing about it on the news. Edward had found a report a few days ago of a running gun battle between the Bloods and the Crips that he thought could be a cover story. But the question remained—was the doctor telling the truth? Had a team of Atlanteans cured her, or had it really been the same people who had given her the stroke to begin with?

Otto realized the others in the Atlantis Allegiance would ask the same questions. Yuhle had already decided she was telling the truth before they got here. Vivian and Edward suspected it might be a trap, and Grunt was convinced it was. If they brought her back to Nevada, her mere presence would split the Atlantis Allegiance into suspicious factions.

Dr. Yamazaki plunked some money on the table for her own meal and smiled. "It will be good to see everyone again. Let's get out of here."

Otto allowed himself a sigh of relief. It looked as though this wasn't a trap after all. If they hadn't been busted yet, they probably wouldn't be. The feds could have blocked off the whole neighborhood and arrested them by now. She would still have to answer a million questions, but first, it was time to hit the road. Once they were back in Nevada, there would be plenty of time for an interrogation.

He looked at her more closely. So this was the scientist who had discovered the Atlantis gene. He was dying to ask her all about it. Now he could finally learn more about Jaxon.

As they walked to the door, they were both so busy scanning the street for the police that they didn't notice the waitress pass by and brush the edge of Dr. Yamazaki's trench coat. Even if they had, they would have barely noticed the tiny patch of clear plastic with a little spider's web of circuits and wires. Once it was on the fabric of the coat, it was all but invisible.

# Chapter 19

JUNE 18, 2016, LOS ANGELES,
CALIFORNIA

1:10 PM

Jaxon was having the least pathetic birthday party of her life. It was also the biggest. She had a grand total of one friend there.

If she thought about it, the whole thing would have made her depressed. There she was, with a birthday cake in the kitchen that said an age that might not be true for a day that almost certainly wasn't, surrounded by foster parents, two instructors, and one friend. The fact that this was the closest thing she'd ever had to a normal birthday party—one where the birthday girl was surrounded by heaps of friends and real family members—should have been enough to make her curl up in a ball and weep.

Kids with summer birthdays always complained that most of their friends were away and they couldn't have a proper party. Having a summer birthday was a small mercy for Jaxon, because it kept her from having to explain to the people in whatever school she was in that year why no one was invited to her parties.

But Jaxon wouldn't allow herself to think about those things. She had spent enough of her life being depressed. She wanted to feel good for a change. It sure helped that Ginger Edwards had managed to come. Jaxon couldn't believe her luck.

They all sat in the backyard, where her foster parents had set up some lawn chairs. A banner strung across the back door said Happy Birthday, and there was a table with healthy snacks and a small pile of presents. Everyone was chatting and drinking Isadore's awesome smoothies.

Jaxon was surprised that Marquis and Juliette had shown up. She'd never seen a teacher at a birthday party before. She hoped the Grants weren't paying them to come, but she didn't mind too much that they were there. While Marquis was a bit too intense, Juliette made for good company. She was very chilled out and had already made good friends with Ginger.

Marquis looked a bit awkward, as though he didn't go to many parties. Even so, he was chatting with the Grants and made pleasant conversation with Jaxon too.

Isadore gave Jaxon one of her stiff hugs. This one lasted longer than usual. "Having a good party?"

"Yeah," Jaxon replied, and she was.

"Well, next year it will be ten times as big. You're going to stay with us. No more moving around for you."

"That's right." Stephen nodded. "We're going to make sure you get the education you need and the stability you deserve."

A lump welled up in Jaxon's throat. She swallowed and said, "Um, I got to go to the bathroom. Back in a sec." She hurried back into the house, wiping her eyes once she was out of sight of everyone else.

"Might as well use it since I'm here," she muttered, going to the bathroom and closing the door behind her.

The downstairs bathroom was typical of the Grants' elegant but minimalist style. The walls and fixtures were all white like the rest of the house, which made Jaxon feel as if she was living inside an aspirin. The only splash of color in the bathroom came from a fern in a white pot sitting on the windowsill. The bright green plant practically glowed in contrast to the whiteness of everything else. The sound of laughter from the party filtered in through the open window.

Jaxon smiled. That party was for her.

She noticed a dead leaf sitting next to the plant, and she grabbed it to chuck it out the window. A tingling went through her fingers. The brown leaf started turning green, fresh color radiating from where her fingers touched.

Jaxon flinched, and the leaf fluttered onto the windowsill. The outline of her finger was clearly visible as a green patch on the otherwise brown, dead leaf.

Peering at it, she saw that that part was alive again.

A shudder passed through her. How the hell did she do that?

She turned to go, heart beating fast as though she were being chased by a ghost. Then she stopped, her hand motionless on the doorknob.

That quote from the Gnostic Gospels popped into her head. "If you let what is inside of you out of you, what is inside of you will save you. If you don't let what is inside of you out of you, what is inside of you will kill you."

She looked back at the leaf that she had started to bring back to life and nodded. "All right, I'll figure this out. I've been keeping enough secrets for so long, I can keep this one too. No point in hiding it from myself though."

Jaxon walked over to the windowsill and reached for the leaf. It skittered across the windowsill and into her hand. Her heart flip-flopped.

*That was the breeze. The window is open, and a breeze blew the leaf in my hand.*

She didn't feel a breeze and decided to ignore that fact. Holding the dead leaf between two fingers, she focused on it. Green life spread from her touch and transformed the curled-up, dry leaf into a living thing once more. Jaxon studied the plant and found where the leaf had dropped off. One stem on the side was brown and wilted. She ran her finger along it, and it sprang to life.

"Let's see how far this can go," she said.

Pressing the base of the leaf against the end of the stem and holding it on with two fingers, she concentrated, imagining the leaf reattached to the plant. After a moment, she took her hand away and gasped.

The leaf and stem were reunited as if they had never died.

Suddenly she felt tired. It wasn't over-whelming, more like she had just run up a long flight of steps, but the effort of reviving the fern had taken some energy out of her.

"Well, looks like I won't be saving the rainforest with the touch of my fingers!" She chuckled, looked at her handiwork, and smiled. This was nothing to be ashamed of.

Jaxon rejoined the party.

"Open your presents!" Ginger said, edging her chair closer as Jaxon sat down. "I love presents, even if I'm not the one getting them."

"All right," Jaxon laughed. She picked up one that was wrapped in black paper embossed with gold Asian dragons. She looked at Marquis. "Is this from you?"

Marquis grinned. "Yeah, I guess it's easy to tell."

"Aw, you didn't have to get me anything," Jaxon said, touched. She opened it and found a book. Jaxon spent a minute puzzling through the title and author so she didn't embarrass herself. "*The Art of War* by Sun Tzu."

"It's as much a philosophy text as a military manual," Marquis explained.

"Um, thanks."

"Open mine now, Jaxon," Juliette said. Her yoga instructor pushed another gift in Jaxon's direction.

Jaxon smiled at her and opened it. Another book. Had these people forgotten she was dyslexic?

She worked through the title. *"The Tao of Pooh."*

"It's actually pronounced 'dow.' It might help you in your spiritual path. Bet you didn't know Winnie the Pooh was a spiritual master, did you?" Juliette said.

Jaxon laughed. At least this one had cute pictures. Next came Stephen and Isadore's gift, a small rectangular package that sat at the center of the coffee table. *I hope this isn't another book. I won't be finished reading them all until my next birthday.*

To her surprise, it was a set of gardening DVDs.

"We'll loan you a computer so you can watch those," Stephen said. "You really have a green thumb."

Jaxon smiled at him. *You have no idea.*

She had saved Ginger's gift for last. It turned out to be a beautiful dress.

"Got to look your best at school," Ginger said before kissing Jaxon's cheek.

"Wow, this is great! Actually, they make us wear uniforms."

Ginger's eyebrows wiggled. "Well, la-di-da!"

The two girls laughed and embraced.

Isadore came out of the back door with a large cake with seventeen candles, and everyone sang "Happy Birthday."

"Make a wish," Isadore said.

*I wish I belonged somewhere.* Jaxon blew out the candles.

"One more year until you're eighteen," Ginger said, nudging her. "Then you'll be a legal adult and can do whatever you want."

That reminder hit Jaxon like a bucket of cold water. She only had a year in this home. She had just gotten here, had just begun to feel comfortable, and soon she'd be moving on.

To what? University? She didn't know if the Grants would pay for it or even what she would study. If she didn't go to college, what would she do? She could always get a job. Would that make her happy, or would she still be lonely and different? Everyone always talked about getting out of school without realizing that entering the real world didn't solve any problems—it only changed them.

Jaxon watched Isadore cutting up the cake and felt as if she were seeing it from a million miles away. Then she snapped out of it. That was the old Jaxon gnawing away at her insides. She was going to be different now.

Okay, the cake was some macrobiotic blob made with locally sourced brown sugar and free-range, cruelty-free eggs, and it tasted like tofu that had been watered down with Ovaltine, but Isadore had slaved in the kitchen all morning to make it for her.

Jaxon looked around at all the smiling faces. Sure, her one friend lived in another city and all the adults at her party were weirdos. Was that so bad? They were here, weren't they? They were chowing down on cake and had brought presents and were actually spending time with her. When was the last time a roomful of people had done that?

Hey, even Marquis was there. Just a few days ago, she had smacked him during practice. Jaxon still got shivers when she thought of the animalistic fury in his eyes when she had hit him. But was that so surprising? She'd made a lucky hit, and he had been taken by surprise by her unusual strength. Being a martial artist, of course he had responded with hostility. Who wouldn't?

But he obviously didn't hold a grudge, seeing as how he had shown up on his day off and even brought a present. It was a lame present, but at least he had brought one. He didn't have to do that. And Marquis was giving her something even better. He was teaching her how to defend herself. If those strange men ever came back, she'd kick their asses even more than she had last time.

But maybe she wouldn't need to. How would they even know she was in Los Angeles? Her name wasn't on any bills or anything, so unless they could get into her sealed CPS files, they'd have no way to find out where she was.

Yes, she thought as she looked around, *maybe I have finally found a place where I belong, a place where people care about me.* She smiled with renewed confidence.

She was safe here.

## About the Author

S.A. Beck lives in sunny California. When she's not surfing, knitting or daydreaming in a hammock, she's writing novels.